Kirkus Review

Two men reflect on what went right and wrong during their long lives in this novel. Widower Jerry, 85, has trouble meeting male friends in Macrobia, his California retirement community. It might have something to do with Macrobia's population being 75 percent female. He meets Walter, 86, in the community's philatelist club. Walter has a unique interest: He only collects stamps from nations that no longer exist. (Jerry opts for stamps from small countries in Europe and Asia.) The two begin a friendship based largely around conversation. Topics include the development of retirement communities, careers, hometowns, travel, and, inevitably, family. "They don't write," gripes Walter about his six kids, "don't post mail; instead, once in a while, one of them tweets. Email is old fashioned, one of them told me." Jerry's own children include an estranged daughter that he abandoned to dodge the Korean War draft by fleeing to Canada; they haven't seen each other in 60 years. Underlying every subject, sometimes explicitly and sometimes not, is the greater one: They are old men, at the end of their lives, awaiting a final epiphany. What did they do right? What did they do wrong? What, in the end, really matters? In this "Old Adult" novel, Foyt (*Marcel Proust in Taos*, 2013, etc.) writes from the perspective of Jerry, whose believable voice is equal parts wistfulness, remorse, and detachment: "I admitted to myself that I had always wanted to underline my thoughts. I mean, I had always admired Matilda and her skills in writing her columns. I did think my thoughts were valid. But for me to share them with strangers?" There isn't much here in the way of plot. Indeed, the climactic moment is something of a deus ex machina, more befuddling than cathartic. Even so, the author has constructed an elegant—and at times compelling—Socratic dialogue on growing very old. These two men of the Silent Generation might not confront any of the really intriguing issues—from their white maleness to the sex lives of octogenarians—but they do hit the classics: parenthood, accomplishments, and the point of it all.

A philosophical tale about two men in old age.

Jon Foyt

The Third Half of Our Lives
Two Old Guys Not Selling Anything

A Novel by Jon Foyt

Andrew Benzie Books
Martinez, California

Published by Andrew Benzie Books
www.andrewbenziebooks.com

Copyright © 2019 Jon Foyt
www.jonfoyt.com

Printed in the United States of America
First Edition: May 2019

10 9 8 7 6 5 4 3 2 1

Foyt, Jon
The Third Half of our Lives: Two Old Guys Not Selling Anything

ISBN: 978-1-950562-05-3

Cover and book design by Andrew Benzie
www.andrewbenziebooks.com
Cover photo ©2000 by Nikos Economopoulos,
Magnum Photos, Ganadio Village, Epirus (Greece)

Dedicated to Helen, always;

and to the Men of Rossmoor:
Jim Wisner, Sam Mataraso, Al Drachman, Bob Tunnell;

plus Maxine Hong Kingston and other supportive friends
for their valuable encouragement and comments.

CONTENTS

PREFACE

Despite this book's alternate title, it is a novel for women and men alike.

There comes a time in our life when we realize we are aging. The realization may come at age 50, more likely 65, most certainly at age 75. By 85, the concept of aging will likely dominate our lives—men and women "of age."

When such realization occurs, life begins to change. Whether or not we move into retirement geograpihically or mentally, or continue working for a living, we notice things: those around us change, we change, everything changes.

In a retirement community, aren't each of us in the same boat, rowing across tranquil seas, the sparkling golden seas, into the glorious sunset. Yet we must ask: is such a perceived nirvana naïve?

*   *   *

The Chorus of Aging

Greek dramas included a chorus of men and boys singing at intervals to explain and add musical perspective to a play. Eons later, a modern-day Chorus of Aging, with written and spoken thoughts, allows viewers and readers, both young or old, to peer into the geriatric drama being staged before their eyes and ears.

At some point in our contemporary aging lives, the Chorus sings more regularly, its notes touching upon balance and the fear of falling. It monitors our pains, new or ongoing. It encourages curiosity, may evoke dread. For sure, it shocks us with the ills of others, even their eventual passing. Death summons older, younger, those we've known, and complete strangers. Mourning, we fill the voids they leave.

The Chorus may comment on a doctor's office visit: what did the MD really say? Will the new prescription offer relief from pain or allay a new uncertainty? What did those tests really tell me? The Chorus may give rise to a fresh dilemma. We may long for a spiritual healer as we seek guidance for the clamor of our increasing concerns.

Yet, like the proverbial elevator music, the Chorus of Aging continues playing, keeping us company against loneliness, soothing our pain, attempting to resolve our unknowns. (Or, perhaps, reminding us of those forces riding piggyback on our lives? The tunes may seem unfamiliar... different... strange.).

PROLOGUE
RETIRING IN MACROBIA

As the focal point of the 15,000-strong Macrobia Active Adult Retirement Village, a copse of Golden Raintrees displays cascading yellow flowers. The trees lovingly encircle the bubbling "Ponce de Leon Fountain of Youth," a scene not unlike the original 1546 painting by Lucas Cranach the Elder, minus the swimmers. Together, the grove and fountain serve as the highlight of the large Macrobian landscape. As a resident, I, Jerry, have come to embrace a certain spirituality about the place where I live. Here, I experience a sense of eternity, possibly more satisfying, a feeling of tranquility that suggests something great beyond life's traditional treasured manifestations. Perhaps like Cranach's canvas, the scene depicts for me the many familiar seniors with whom I interact, those who in their advancing lives, call Macrobia their "Home."

Today, during the publicized Annual Festivities Week, displays of residents' craft works dangle by colorful cords from the branches of the tallest Raintrees, large signs invite new residents to come to the Newcomers Orientation Program and Wine Tasting. "Learn about our many activities and meet club members."

*   *   *

On my early morning walk this morning and, as always alone with my thoughts, I admired the sunny flowers of the Raintrees. Some time ago, when I had passed the test to gain admittance to this community, I had learned that the Raintree was originally from Korea, brought to Europe in the 17th century, or were the seeds originally from China? I've forgotten by now, but no matter. But I do fully recall that Thomas Jefferson, later on, imported the seeds from a Paris garden, and the trees flourished in Virginia.

Over time and along with everything else, the Raintree spread westward across North America, stopping long enough in Indiana to have a county named after it. Oh, that was only in literature—Ross Lockridge's reflective Civil War novel from years back that I've read, and the ensuing movie with Elizabeth Taylor that my late wife, Matilda, and I watched. Today the Raintree is a favorite of landscape architects, evidence my Macrobia retirement community's arboretum-like environment.

Ambling through the Raintrees, I came upon my friend Walter. With his ivory-tipped cane, he was pointing toward his own Stamp Club display that hung from a large tree branch. Swinging in the light breeze, the multi-colored stamps invited further examination.

On a table below, the Book Club offered copies of resident authors' published works. While on another branch, digital compositions of the Photography Club's dangled, surrounded by samplings from the Art Cub's members' oils, watercolors, and etchings from members of the Art Club. My, what an impressive showing of older folks' talents, I mused, appreciating the scene.

Earlier, Walter and I had met shortly after I had moved to Macrobia and attended a Stamp Club meeting. Walter was then serving as the Club president. This morning he called out to me, "Jerry, come see my collection of dead country stamps." He smiled, his mustache vibrating as it does when he has something of importance to relate. I smiled in return as I approached my friend. "Jerry, my dead countries didn't stay around long. As you can see, I've outlived them all." He then paused to ask, "Did you know that those ancient Macrobians back in 500 BC hung around for a lifespan of 120 years before they went stage left, or so Herodotus tells us? The Greek says they drank water from a fountain with some sort of rejuvenating powers. Must have been just like ours here."

I hadn't read up on yesteryear's Greek historians, so I didn't know, but in my brief but deep friendship with Walter, I knew if he knew, then I now knew. So, I asked, "My friend, are you here for a lifespan of such a reported duration? And if so, may I ask, does such a contemplation tell us about you?"

Walter laughed heartily, a trait I found endearing, and replied, "If I live as long as those Macrobians, I'll be the oldest living specimen in this place."

"You'd win the longevity prize for sure, I'd venture."

This time, Walter laughed even more expressively. "Yes, and maybe I'll attract more retirees to join our Stamp Club." Walter displayed a warm smile on his gray bearded face. His trusty cane was by his side, and he wore a leather elbow-patched corduroy jacket, rendering him a picture-perfect philatelist.

*   *   *

By this time at Macrobia, I had attended a number of Stamp Club meetings where, among other things, I talked about my own stamp collection, which, like Walter's, was also specialized. Mine however, focused on small countries, namely those lesser-known nations still in existence in Europe and Asia.

Alas my wife Matilda, during our 60-year marriage, had enjoyed her own pursuits, quite apart from collecting stamps. She wrote a column on women's issues for a newspaper syndicate. Our divergence of interests seemed to reflect a not uncommon marriage dichotomy. At one of the Stamp Club meetings I attended, a widow showed up with a cardboard box containing her late husband's stamp collection. Could Walter please accept it, she asked, so she could have more closet space? Or, perhaps he, or the club, might buy the collection from her, or advise her of the collection's worth?

Walter explained that the only available storage space was in his little house, which I knew from spending time there, was as small as my own place, except that his was filled to the ceiling with similar cardboard boxes. He once confided to me that he didn't know what to do with all the collections, other than donate them to a nearby stamp library, where their fate would remain unknown. Yet, once in a while, he acknowledged, there might be something of significant value hidden away in one of the boxes, depending on the husband's collection focus. So, Walter would obligingly take a quick look at a box's contents and let the owner know if a spouse's hobby was a positive exception to the otherwise negative rule.

Occasionally, a member would state emphatically, "Stamp collecting isn't what it used to be in this country. Look back at how things were before young people got their cell phones and computers, and that became their way of learning.

Then Walter might add, "Perhaps today in Europe, stamps may still be a focus for collectors, but not here in the US. Here, back in the 1930s and '40s, stamp collecting was both an attraction and a challenge for us little boys, and even some little girls."

Good at monitoring a meeting, Walter made certain each of us participated in the discussions. He'd go around the room giving everyone a chance to talk about stamps, stamp collecting, our feelings about specific stamps and how stamps had affected our lives, and so on. I marveled at how he encouraged members to speak up and express themselves. One member reminded us, "Collecting stamps was how we learned about geography and each country's rulers." Club members dutifully nodded in nostalgic agreement. Recalling my own youthful excitement, I shared, "It was a time when the world was full of exotic countries whose royalty peered out at us from a country's colorful stamps."

"Still thrills me," a member added. I agreed with her.

One particular day, a club member spoke about the theme of her US collection, which focused on the earliest stamps. "In the beginning, they were not perforated," she reported. "Stamps were cut with a scissors, and people tried to re-use them. So, the postal authorities put hidden marks on stamps so they couldn't be used again."

"Kind of like our lives here," Walter quipped in a whisper to me. "We're marked and can't be used again."

*　　　　*　　　　*

"Well, Walter," I remarked, "You and I are a quite different sort of old guys," I waited, then added, "Maybe stamps have helped us glue our friendship."

Walter agreed, chuckled, showing his warm smile.

It was apparent to me that we each had an innate feeling for stamps, as well as a curiosity about their heritage, and especially about the countries at the times they issued the stamps. As I got to know Walter better, I surmised that his focus on stamps, from what he was calling "dead countries," was in line with the atypical careers he had experienced. From our many conversations, I had learned that my friend had multiple endeavors in his life. Unlike most of the retired men I'd met here in Macrobia (and some women, too) each of whom had long focused careers with big corporations, governments, schools, or non-profits, there was no single career path for Walter. Many of his career ventures, like his countries, had met with dead ends. His stamp collection seemed to mirror his life. This knowledge caused me to worry about Walter. How had he qualified financially to be able to live in Macrobia? I mean, the requirements, including a FICO score above 700, are rather rigid.

I soon knew I wanted to learn more about Walter and his life, and he always seemed interested in knowing more about me.

Chapter 1
Macrobia Retirement Village

"There is a fountain of youth: it is in your mind, your talents, the creativity you bring to your life and the lives of people you love. When you learn to tap this source, you will truly have defeated age."
—*Sophia Loren*

Setting our Macrobia stage, as well as placing present time into historic perspective, I need to mention the *Get Acquainted with Macrobia Retirement Village* booklet that each new resident, including me of course, was required to read. Then came the test to be admitted. In studying the pamphlet, I learned that my newly adopted community was founded in the 1960s. The booklet went on to describe that time when a number of other such communities were being built in California and the Sun Belt states of Florida and Arizona. Several homebuilders and individuals were cited as innovators for the idea of retirement communities. My real estate broker had advised me that it wasn't necessary to remember everyone's name to pass the test, a relief to us both, I'm sure. I have never been good at tests, I told her when we were reviewing the booklet of requirements.

I mean, some people are better at taking tests than others, or so I had consoled myself whenever my test results had come in from attempts in my younger life to qualify for this or that.

On occasion, Walter and I had each embarked upon a mental sojourn when asked by other seniors at some gathering or event to relate how and why both of us got here. At such times, we recited our reasons for relocating.

The stories folks told at these gatherings were each different, yet similar—careers ending, then what? Were children or grandchildren near? Yes. Were the Macrobia facilities attractive, conducive to the golden years. Yes. Were the variety of club activities of interest? Yes. Were the housing prices less than in nearby cities? Usually. Were health facilities conveniently located and affordable? For the most part, Yes.

*   *   *

Macrobia Activities Council

Approaching mid-day, crowds were now gathering in the Golden Raintree grove. Rows of chairs had been brought in to face the fountain of youth. A podium was set up with a microphone and two matching audio speakers.

At noon, the director of the Activities Council, Alicia Gonzalez, addressed the crowd. Popular with residents, she received a round of applause as she began, "It is my pleasure to introduce Rex Kingfish, president of our volunteer Macrobia Board of Directors." More applause as a tall, longhaired man with a full beard relied upon his cane to maneuver the two steps up to the podium.

After Alicia raised the microphone to accommodate his height, Rex began, "I recognize a lot of you from your entry interviews. Welcome everyone.

"I thought I'd take this opportunity for you out there to trace for you the development of places such as Macrobia. Living in a retirement community is, for most of you, a new and—we hope, an exciting experience at this stage in your life."

Rex went on, "Decades ago, for the first time, working people were beginning to think about the possibility of their own retirement—a life beyond age 65, when, as everyone knows, something happened to careers. Most were mandated to end. Previously in America, one's career ending event often signified a final stop to one's lifetime plan. But what if, as rumors circulated, there was another chapter? What if an active retirement could fill the void by offering an epilogue to one's life? This new possibility, with an accompanying active lifestyle, had resulted in the creation of active adult retirement communities like Macrobia lifestyle."

There were nods of agreement from many in the audience. A few people applauded.

Rex went on, "The idea of pensions began with Union Army veterans of the Revolutionary War, continuing on to the Union veterans of the American Civil War. They were entitled to monthly pension checks for their service to the country."

"What about the Confederate soldiers?" I asked in a whisper to Walter.

He shook his head. "Out of luck. Too bad, too, for had they been paid, the rift between North and South might have been healed over before continuing on even today."

Rex continued, "Social Security and Railroad Retirement were already in effect in the early 20th century. And coming down the pike was the promised health care of Medicare for seniors. In the days of the 1950s and 60s, each of these new concepts and promises, for the first time, were now on older peoples' minds." I suggested to Walter, "He needs to mention the growing apprehension—or maybe uncertainty—about the unexplored timeframe of senior retirement."

Walter nodded and whispered back, "The many aspects of retirement are the major questions we here face. Right?"

I wondered if Rex and his Board had that all figured out.

Rex wound up his remarks by saying, "In this life extension concept—given the new statistics detailing increasingly longer life spans—there's a need for individuals to plan for their own life after the retirement party and the proverbial gold watch. Today, this new stage of life offers older folks an exciting horizon, coupled with the need for financial planning."

Alicia thanked him and contributed, "Our financial planning office, headed by Blanche Bouganza, stands ready to advise you all. A meeting with her is included in your monthly homeowner's dues."

More applause. Then people began to circulate among the Raintree's dangling displays and club tables.

CHAPTER 2
LIVING IN RETIREMENT

"When grace is joined with wrinkles, it is adorable.
There is an unspeakable dawn in happy old age."
—Victor Hugo

Through our ongoing conversations, Walter and I discovered that, beyond stamp collecting, we shared another interest: human history and, more specifically, the progress of medicine during our own lifetimes. Reflecting on his own present circumstances, living at Macrobia, Walter observed that retirement was scarcely mentioned in the popular media, including those magazines awaiting patients in doctors' offices.

At our respective ages, we could each remember how things were decades ago. Walter recounted conversations he had overheard from his parents back in Des Moines, talks over dinner, at cocktail parties, after religious services about ideas called retirement. As a kid he had picked up on the excitement stemming from discussions of such unknowns as Social Security and lifetime employee pensions, his parents' hopes and fears about being part of this as yet unwritten history. Such concepts were his parents' hopes, along with fears that they might be left out of the still to be written pages of a retirement lifestyle.

Having lived in Macrobia for several years and having gotten to know a number of seniors, I expressed to Walter my opinion that few people proffered answers or described their plans to cope with unforeseen eventualities in their retirement, be they health or financial.

Walter agreed with my observations, adding that corporate or government retirement plans—which our fellow residents likely had—

would provide some sort of pensions and, possibly, medical coverage. Trouble was, he insisted, the extent of all of retiree's medical and financial needs in their entirety was probably as great and deep as the oceans themselves. And an employer's failure to provide, doom a person with their funds exhausted, to a place among the homeless?

Apart from the money issue, I have found that most of the older folks I have met here were seeking some sort of retirement playbook telling them what to expect and how they might cope with this new and as yet uncharted lifestyle. Call it a virgin landscape. Call it coming of (old) age—call it a new camaraderie of aging. Call it whatever you might, this embryonic unknown of life was now upon them, upon us, upon me. In fact, the volunteer-run Macrobia Library had opened a new shelf situated next to its "Young Adult" books, labeling it "Old Adult."

Browsing the library shelves, I began to wish I had talked more with my parents about their lives, and less about mine. But, as I recall, in those days, you never really got to know your parents, I mean, in a way, their deep attributes you needed to know in order to understand them. And, I realized that my own three kids had never been that interested in their parent' lives, my late wife's and mine.

As I related to Walter in another of our ensuing chats, for my parents, these developments in retirement seemed to make little difference in their lives. Walter allowed as how his parents fit into that same picture, predestined by the actuarial tables to be shorter lives. Except for pining about Benjamin Franklin, Michelangelo, and Lazarus living to a great old age, life was typically over with in the decade from one's 50s to their 60s. There was no need to plan beyond, other than to continue to pursue one's faith in a life everlasting, a belief that from childhood that showed a light at the end of life's tunnel. But today, as Walter pointed out, with our new retirement lifestyles and horizons, that tunnel extended farther and deeper into the mystique of aging.

Progress in life expectancy, Walter continued, had been reserved for those later generations like ours and those of us now living in Macrobia.

Walter, and I with him, lamented, and I readily joined with him, that lacking pensions and health care plans, a lot of people were not so fortunate as to be able to live here where we lived. Many were unable to afford its benefits offered—those derived from lifestyle progress and medical science developments. But, progress should be for all, don't you think, I asked Walter. Alas, I thought, where does one's responsibility for others stop? Or does it? Walter admitted he didn't know, nor did I, but we had each identified retirement as a major cultural dichotomy. So, how do those not so financially fortunate fend when they can no longer work and be gainfully employed? How do they pay for their own retirement? Or do they?

That evening, I felt a mixture of happiness blended with sorrow. Walter wasn't around, so I slept on the dilemma and awoke the next morning, happy to be alive, happy to be where I was and remain and happy with myself. Still, the suffering of others less fortunate than I in their golden years troubled me.

∗　　　∗　　　∗

Our Resident Population

Every year, I learned from Walter, members of the Macrobia Statistics Club undertake a population analysis. They dub their report covering the 15,000 residents "Census Tidbits." They have fun analyzing the population by compiling the community's ever-changing demographics. Well, I thought, if that makes them happy, then good for them and good for us, too, because by studying their reports, we will become better informed about the makeup of our adopted community.

I remember some of the data in their latest report. It showed the median age of Macrobia residents, after all the number crunching, to be 76.2. That's young, I thought to my self, 10 years younger than me. The gender breakdown stood at something around 75 per cent female—the exact figure I've forgotten. The club president said it was pretty much in line with the national stats for senior brackets.

∗　　　∗　　　∗

To review, I'm Jerry, 86, and he's Walter, 86—I think that's his age. Maybe he told me once, but if he did I've forgotten and, besides, in this place one's age blends into the days and weeks that float past, forming a comfort of camaraderie, a daily rolling-in fog of age with its assumed, aware-to-all misty attributes. Besides, birthdays occur often—there's always someone with one. So, you learn to remember those passing-go mile markers. Maybe it is because everyone talks about them, and on the other hand, no one talks about them.

Birthdays are a time for humorous sort-of celebratory cards. The nearby supermarket has a special marked shelf (displayed in large type) showing off zany old-age birthday greeting cards. The card makers must rake in a fortune from folks like us who buy them to give friends a laugh, a long, but brief specific type of laugh that is soon spent and promptly stowed away for, hopefully, another 12 months.

Some cards play a tune. Some others may be accompanied by a trio of local high school a cappella singers arriving at the recipient's home where they joyously harmonize a birthday wish. To me and to many I've heard from, such birthday greetings are a nagging reminder of our advancing age, a time of continuously adding to, or maybe subtracting from, our anticipated years.

We seniors, Walter has reminded me more than once, are growing older every day, like it or not. But at Macrobia, most people seem to accept the retirement life—that is, growing older and older among like-minded classmates in the kindergarten school of aging, a learning environment where every diploma is an advanced degree. This, Walter advised me, is the game plan for the lot of us here—we who disembarked from the younger ship of life at this landing, hoping to enjoy the life of retirement—whatever it is. Walter once confessed he didn't have a textbook definition of the word, so he encouraged me to work with him toward crafting an acceptable description of retirement. I accepted his challenge, and one day over beers, we tried, but I can't remember our agreed-upon definition. A week later I asked Walter what it was, and he'd forgotten, too. He said he'd written it down somewhere….

CHAPTER 3
WHERE IS HOME?

"In youth we learn, in age we understand."
—Marie von Ebner-Eschenbach

Curious to find out if there were any other residents living in Macrobia from my home state, male or female, or couples, with whom I might make friends, I asked a member of the Statistics Club about the home states of residents, mentioning mine.

At my query, she blurted out, "Indiana?" She quickly added, "Hoosiers go south to Florida—the West Coast of Florida," she spoke as if she had taken a census, which I figured she probably had, because as I thought about it, all my Midwest relatives had gone south to Florida—the West Coast, that is. Those retirees from New York and such other eastern places had gone south to Florida—the East Coast. I think they never met, even later on, during their coastal sunset years sipping orange juice and sunshine. She admonished me, "You took the wrong train or plane, mister." So, there were no fellow folks from South Bend, Terra Haute, or even Wabash, let alone Bloomington. I won't go through the highway atlas of town names. She was going on about stats as if, by reading the reported numbers in one of her club's reports, one could get a compendium of Macrobian facts. But, who's going to remember all that?

I asked, "How about Kentucky?" only to get a derisive laugh as she mumbled something about how she always wanted to be a jockey up at Churchill Downs, and then she turned and walked away.

"Hey, wait a minute," I called out. "I want to know."

"Read one of the addendums in the back of the report," she instructed.

I did, and there was my name, the only name from a place I'd pretty well forgotten about called Indiana. A long time go, I told myself. Even if I were to go back there today, it wouldn't be the same as I remembered it, would it?

I queried Walter as to his concept of home.

"I've had so many," he replied, so I can give you a mixed bag of answers."

I learned that during his life, Walter had moved about like the little white ball in a pinball machine, a fun device most of us could recall playing as teenagers, hour after hour.

I told him, "One home town for me," as if I'd failed the exam of life and couldn't come up with an excuse.

Yet naming a hometown was a compelling question. I kept badgering myself with why it was so important among my fellow senior residents. I asked myself if one's home base in life—where you started out on life's journey—was a concept? Perhaps it was not a specific place, not even a house, and not, as my late wife Matilda and I used to call it, "The Old Home Place?"

After thinking about the question of where one was from, the answer I came up with was that time moves on in our lives, and each of us seniors is here now, today, all 15,000 of us in Macrobia. Where we're from no longer makes a difference, that is, until you find yourself talking to somebody from New York. I detect, and maybe I'm just overly sensitive—and Walter says sometimes I am—that there's a mien about those New York folks that they're from the best of all places, and if we'll just stop the clock from turning and the earth from rotating, the warm snowless and iceless days will sooner or later come back. That's when they will all reel back there like a yo-yo attached to its retrievable string.

So, in the Macrobia statistical report, the list of those from New York filled ten pages, second only to the list from California, which was almost endless.

The subject still troubled me, and I related my concern to Walter. He thought about it for a while. Sometimes Walter would not respond right away, sitting there like a mother hen as if he were hatching a response. Sometime later he did reply, "Whyzzit so important to you? Geography of origin, I mean?" He went on, "I mean, look at the cv's of the people here, that is, those who reveal their curricula vita. Some of these folks have been all over the world, many assigned to live in the remotest of remotes or the busiest of business centers in their careers." Walter posed the question, "What is home for them? Some airline terminal in Malaysia they've passed through 100 times, so they know every bar, every restroom, every bookstore, every gift shop, every duty free?"

Some days I think Walter is imbued with scads of wisdom. I wish I'd accumulated as much. Maybe, I speculated, with his checkerboard career path and his dwelling on countries that didn't make it in the world, he was more in tune with what worked and what didn't work in life, and in the world. I marveled at his acumen, and wished I could draw upon such a reservoir of street smarts.

As to the dilemma of where is home, I was giving up on any attachment to Matilda's and my old home state, and on the town where she and I had grown up and met, our high school years and later our separate colleges, and then the career days we lived together, she raising three children—well, me, too—and I working in my career job. We'd always come back there, for the stops on my career were like stage appearances in a traveling thespian parade of places.

But now, by myself, I was here in Macrobia. This is my home now. I am on my own, after all those what now, in retrospect, seemed to be false starts. One thing for sure, I wasn't going to go down the road of humiliation again by mentioning Indiana. Better I say Mars, if and when asked. No, better I say New York, except I don't have the accent or the mannerisms. But wait, I do have an accent. We all do, don't we? I mean, dialects and mannerisms. If you're a linguist, you can guess, usually pretty accurately where someone is from, just by how they talk and pronounce certain words and the manner in which they express themselves. Just listen to the way in which I talk about doing the warshing, or the local woman we once elected to represent us in Warshington, DC.

*   *   *

I recalled the evening Walter and I chatted away in his little one bedroom home. It was, as were all the homes here, including my little place, the home one now lived in, following homes one had lived in during earlier lives. The previous homes were big or small, owned or rented, pristine or dilapidated, simple or elegant. But they had been home. Now home was here, wherever it was physically located in the expanse of Macrobia. There were areas of lower priced and areas of higher priced homes. As with all real estate, values varied with location and condition.

In Walter's home, when he first invited my visit, I had observed that along two walls the shelves equaled his height of a little less than six feet on down to knee-high. Reminded me of a time long ago when each of us, as was everyone in Macrobia, as tall as knee-high. Forget the grasshopper reference, for there are none in Macrobia—in fact, virtually no flying or crawling things of that sort, for like in a hospital, spraying disinfectants seemed to be the menu of the day, along with an array of bug repellants distributed seemingly everywhere by the outside contractor. The contractor has a regular schedule, so knowing his timeline, and being about, you could avoid breathing in the poisons.

On Walter's shelves, he displayed many of his stamps, visible so that each visitor, were they interested—and one couldn't call on Walter for any length of time and not be interested—would admire them. They were not tucked away or hidden in a formal collector's book to be opened, searched for and then squinted at under a magnifying glass. These were out in plain site as if they were an artist's collection—engraved art adorning the shelves. I thought to myself it was art that was really adorning Walter. Interspersed were books and articles about his collected countries, names that were no more, except in the historic past—books about their stories, their people, their cultures, their former place on earth. Walter was like a museum curator, as each country was labeled using consistent font on the edge of the shelf displaying the country, well, that is the former country. The font represented Walter, bold and in italics.

CHAPTER 4
GETTING TO KNOW ME

Ah! Sweet mystery of life
At last I've found thee
Ah! I know at last the secret of it all;
All the longing, seeking, striving, waiting, yearning
—Rida Johnson Young and Victor Herbert

Unlike the women—how would I know?—to us Macrobia men, expensive, stylish, rugged attire no longer connotes our status among other males. Nor is it any longer intended to impress persons of the other gender. No more does our displayed fashion rank our societal position, like stars on a general's uniform. Once ensconced in Macrobia, it is not important to suggest to viewers how successful we are, or were, or aspire to be, or claim to be.

Most of us males dress casual, unless we are—and I am not— among the serious dancers. That's when those in the Penguin Club put on their twice-a-year formal ballroom dancing attire—gowns and tuxedos—and shuffle across the polished hardwood dance floor. I don't have a tux anymore. I sold it in the sale we held after Matilda passed away. I sent some of her things to our daughter, but the rest of her mother's belongings and a lot of mine were sold—my downsizing that allowed me to fit into the small Macrobia place I bought. Why would I need more space for a lot of old things from our marriage of years ago that I don't look at or use anymore? Those were the questions I had asked myself and posed to the realtor who found the little home for me here. Walter told me he never did own a tux.

Following my wife's passing and after moving here, along with my talking with other retired people, have urged me onward in my desire, living alone as a widower, to feel ennobled to embark upon a quest to understand my own mind and feel comfortable with my own emotions. I decided I must become intimately acquainted with my own self. For my life's customary supportive guidance and direction, alas, I no longer heeded Matilda's feminine voice telling me, suggesting in her own way, guiding in her wisdom, her input affecting how I lived life, charting my course and envisioning my personal— and ours together—goals. Now I am on my own. As a result, I am finding myself struggling with the chores and dilemmas of day-to-day life. So, I have decided to try to understand myself. If I'm going to live with myself, and not be within the rules and confines of a daily marriage, then I better get to know myself, perhaps in the same way as I think I knew my late wife.

Listening, often in silence, to others, married and single, divorced and widowed, female and male, offers me some insights into the values and personalities of other people as they paint their own candid picture of their lives, revealing their own selves. I have asked myself—and sometimes them—if values have changed now that we are living day after day in this retirement community? Or have our values been rigidly fixed, cast in bronze through the history of our own experiences, sculpted by trial and error from experiences during our younger, or even more recent pre-retirement lives?

In monitoring my fellow seniors, I have heard the individual stories from their yesteryears. In so doing, I have tried to bring out other seniors, prod them to talk and tell, to share their emotions, and opine their wisdom.

I know one is thought to have acquired wisdom from experience, from advice received, from counsel offered and honored, and from each of life's learning situations. Maybe those sometimes brief and sometimes prolonged moving life picture frames in my earlier life have now come to help me to see myself in more depth, as a more rounded character rather than the crude stick figure I may have felt about myself after Matilda's passing. I found I was craving a more advanced and deeper perspective on myself. I talked to Walter about my quest to find the self and why I thought the search was becoming important to me. Suggesting that maybe I was overly curious, he did think for a while about my quest. Finally, he urged me on.

One day in my quest for wisdom, I realized that during most of my life I had been ensconced in a family situation—first my youth and my parents—their family (and mine, too)—then school and a fraternity (their family and mine) in college, followed by my own family with Matilda and our three children. But now it was simply me—my own family self, and that's that, except for my new friends, especially Walter.

In hindsight, the major changes to my history of rather comfortable family scenarios had seemingly happened all of a sudden. Thinking back, one day the treasured time with the succession of family times was behind me. Leading their own lives, our children had left the nest and were no longer close by. Matilda had passed away. Now I was ensconced in a retirement community. Here, everyone has a different life story, unique in geography, special in their unique chapters as they covet their own lifestyles… yet all seeming to blend together, to seem so alike in their parallel storylines. Or so, in my mind, was this abstract canvas of retired life shaping up.

To grasp my role in this broader societal landscape was now of utmost importance. That is, if I was to fully understand myself and apply understanding and compassion to the many life stories around me, including my own self.

The other day, I realized I was trying to transfer my learned and well-executed (so I judged) prior responsibilities of family and career to shape them so they would apply to this place. Where, I queried at two AM one morning, was my family? Was it here? No, I cautioned, it was not here. Or was it? I felt as if I was asking life's TV crew to run a re-play of my life. The "booth upstairs" would decree its finding. Was I the booth? Was Walter? Or was it not a booth, but instead some spiritual authority ensconced up there atop an all-knowing platform in a layer above the private boxes in the stadium of life? Was this ultimate authority, in its rippling robes of importance, waiting there, reviewing the life in which I have been a suited-up player? Was the "booth" about to deliver a verdict on my life? As part of its assignment, was it going to cast a judgment on all the other seniors here in Macrobia? And on those who, once upon a time, were here, and maybe in spirit still are? Was that fair? Was that realistic? Could I avoid this pseudo-judgment day? I searched my lifetime experiences for answers, if there were answers. Pondering, the instructions I soon gave myself was to focus my quest, I must find and then try to understand my true self.

But then I wondered what did it matter to me, or to anyone else, what someone or someone's higher authority had to say in judgment of my life? I mean, I had lived my life, and done it well, I suppose, at least by the standards imposed at the time, the rules of the game of life, or living, of confirming, of excelling, of dedicating yourself to family, as the game of male life was played at the time. So, even if there is criticism now, from someone here or some authority, what does it matter to me, to anyone?

Maybe today, my kids and perhaps their kids might demean my life as irrelevant in the scheme of things, as it relates to what in their minds is currently important; that is, what the authorities—the role models—tweet on their tablet, or what information comes up on the screen of their cell phones. The fact that I can remember—no, more than remember, I can still feel the vibes from the people dragged into World War II, in the fighting, on the home front, in the boot camps, the death and despair, the hopelessness of battle, and then the feel, the thrill, the reward of final victory. I can sense the deep importance of the civil rights movement. I can appreciate the day after day manual work that farmers labored with when this country was primarily agricultural. I can live sacrifices of parents for their kids so they might have the money and the encouragement to go to college—perhaps the first in their families to do so, and how unusual that was in those dim days of yesteryear.

But all that is water under the bridge, as they say, times past, lost and forgotten, long ago past, today of little or no note. Yet not really forgotten, at least by me. So then what is important from those days, to me, to my children, to my grandchildren?

I started to ask Walter about some of these matters, but I realized he was lost in his stamps, the failed countries and their history, for each of them, albeit short and dead-end. But Walter had been   .

listening to my verbal thoughts. Soon his response was courteous but also unhelpful. I wrestled with my dilemma for days thereafter, without resolution, yet with the ongoing curiosity that age begets.

CHAPTER 5
THE SELF

"The Spirit is the True Self."
—Cicero

S o, what is this thing, the abstract term called "self"? At this stage in my life after all the decades of living, exploring, thinking, learning, traveling, working, raising—or rather helping to raise three kids, don't you think I ought to know? Yet the more I think about it, the more I realize I don't really know what self is.

Over the months since we met, Walter and I have talked about the concept of self. Neither of us, in my opinion, in spite of years of experience being ourselves, for better or worse, can adequately define the word, except to acknowledge, each to each, that we'd like to learn more about what a self really is. Walter, who tells me he has been searching for answers for a long time, keeps advising me to look more into Buddhism for clues about the concept of self. I have come to value Walter's fresh insights. Especially at this age, I always become excited about new ideas and new approaches to life and its mysteries. I occasionally recall the lyrics of "Ah, Sweet Mystery of Life."

So, I reasoned that maybe in that Eastern philosophy of Buddhism, adapted in recent years, as Walter explained, to enter the American spiritual culture, I might find answers. Except, the closer I think I'm getting to an answer, the more important the quest becomes and the broader is the need for a more inclusive answer.

Perhaps, Walter suggested one evening at his place, the longer we live, the more intimate we will become with vital in-depth questions coming to us from the present, but based on the past, while gelling thoughts for the future, and hopefully find ourselves enjoying hints of answers for the present. Mulling over what he just told me, Walter went on to advise that this relatively new philosophy—at least in our Western culture—once he got into it, had helped him in coming to terms with the memories of his earlier career shortcomings, the failures, the re-tries, and his few successes. That is, he said, "In my trying to understand them and put them in a mindful perspective."

His words caused me to press, asking, "The concept of the self is in our minds, wouldn't you say?"

He frowned. Then nodded.

I went on, "Then, how does the body affect the self?"

"Now we're into health—bodily health." It was a statement.

My turn to nod, causing me to ask, "Prostate?"

"Been there."

"How'd it affect your self?"

Walter looked agitated, then calming, he told me, "In time, I came to terms with the medical diagnosis, but that took a while. My self was supportive of the medical people… their biopsies… followed by the Gleeson scores…."

"What'd you do?"

"Not me, the radiation, the treatments."

"And?"

"Gone… the cancer… so far." He added, "Now my PSA is way low. You?"

I recited some statistics about the percentage of men who have enlarged prostates.

"Affects almost all men," Walter said, agreeing with me. "And you? Now that you've brought it up, and I've told you, now you tell me."

I declined.

He fumed.

I relented, telling him, "Out damned spot, like Macbeth."

"Witches don't have one."

I teased, "How do you know?"

He grew serious. "Side effects?"

"You got it. Still have."

"Me, too."

"I'd never do it again."

"Guy, you only got one."

"Had," I said, wanting to change the subject.

CHAPTER 6
A DIFFERENT APPROACH

Walter had told me at one time in his life, while pursuing one of his many careers, he was a board-certified psychologist. That was when he encouraged me to pursue a different set of answers by looking into a discipline known as evolutionary psychology.

"What's that?" I blurted, thinking I'd need to look up the discipline in one of Darwin's books. Maybe it meant something weird. Of course, sometimes I did think Walter was a little weird. And, like me, probably he is. But then, as if to explain the concept, he said, "You see, Jerry, we're all—each of us—imbued, or maybe burdened, with what went before us in our family lineage—that is, the DNA framework charting each of our lives as we came into this world. The idea traces each of us, given our ethnicities, to those of our lineage who went before us—parents, grandparents, and so on. Unbeknownst to us, the evolution of our psychological makeup affects our emotions today, and may have triggered our personalities, our makeup, our outlook on life. It's all tucked away up here." He pointed to his head. "It governs our individual selves, shapes our personalities, influences our emotions, directs our behavior, role-plays our interactions with other people." Walter went on to insist, "In analyzing anyone, especially yourself, this evolutionary background can't be overlooked."

"Oh, come on, Walter," I said. "It's what we learned or felt by age six. That's what makes us who we are." I've always believed that, and now Walter was suggesting, no, telling me, I had been running on the wrong track all my life. I had to let that sink in, and did.

Soothingly, Walter said I could continue to believe that, because that's what most people believed, but if I wanted to be out in front of the pack, I could delve into evolutionary psychology. Then he opened his stamp collection and began admiring the issues he owned, leaving me to search my own Funk and Wagnalls, aka Google, for the topic of evolutionary psychology.

CHAPTER 7
MEN TO MATCH MY MOUNTAINS

And the devil, taking him up into a high mountain, shewed unto him
all the kingdoms of the world in a moment of time
—St Luke, 4:5

A book by Irving Stone years ago was entitled: "Men To Match My Mountains." It was about winning the West. Silly, I thought at the time, for to whom were we going to lose the West? Well, one day Walter suggested, it was Mexico because, given the World War I episode of the Zimmerman Telegram wherein Germany promised Mexico to return the lands they gave up in the treaty of Guadalupe-Hidalgo, if they joined Germany and fought for the Central Powers against the Allies. Fat chance but, once it was made public, Walter told about how Woodrow Wilson and most Americans viewed the telegram as a wartime threat. Promptly, our nation and especially the media began to advocate this country entering into The Great War against Germany and the Central Powers.

Yet my take at the time had been that Irving Stone was calling upon us males to match the soaring heights of American mountains, whether it be the Appalachians, the Rockies, the Sierra Nevada, Mount Denali in the Alaska Range, or wherever heights beckoned to be climbed or equaled in male dominance and historic importance. It was each of our male responsibility to excel, and to do so in echoing those soaring national geological heights.

Macrobia had its mountain nearby, not as tall as the others from sea to shining sea, but tall enough to command the surrounding landscape for miles and miles in all directions. In fact, atop this mountain was where Charles Lindbergh planted an airline beacon in the 1920s to light the way for the courageous pilots who were pioneering transcontinental U. S. Air Mail flights for the post office.

Walter said he wanted to climb this mountain, and so I said I'd join him. We retrieved our hiking poles, found our daypacks, bought water bottles, packed a lunch, and set out. The Macrobia hiking club gave us a trail map, and we talked to their leader for advice prior to launching our upward trek.

As we trudged upward, step at a time, poles accompanying us by pointing down at the rocky and dusty trail, I reflected that climbing a mountain was like getting through life. There always seemed to be more uphill than downhill, the trail being sometimes unmarked, sometimes scenic, sometimes dull. But always up, or so the trail and life seemed.

But like our national anthem, "Gave proof through the night that our flag was still there," throughout this day, every time we looked up, the scenery gave proof that our mountain was still there. And so were our lives, offering Walter and me a maybe surmountable, and maybe not, ongoing challenge to conquer what lay ahead.

CHAPTER 8
KNOWING WALTER

How wonderful it is for the soul when—
after so many struggles with lust, ambition, strife, quarreling, and other
passions—these battles are at an end, and it can return to live within itself.
—Marcus Tullius Cicero, 44 BC
"How to Grow Old," by Phillip Freeman, Pepperdine, 2019
Jim Michaels, Wall Street Journal review, January 12-13, 2019

By now, so I had come to surmise, my friend Walter was up front about a lot of what could be considered personal matters. During our times together, he had confided some deep thoughts to me, and I to him. These revelations usually took place on the late afternoons and early evenings when the lure of reminiscing overcame us and dominated our conversation.

We had to remind ourselves that in Macrobia they roll up the sidewalks at 8:30. Well, not literally, of course, but in his retirement community they might as well impose a curfew on age. By being about after that hour, you might alert the security cruiser driver to think you were wandering aimlessly about in a state of dementia, lost from your home, lost in your late hours of life. Nevertheless, after exhausting our chats, Walter and I would part, each hoofing our own way home for another night alone.

While listening to Walter and his personal conversation, albeit confidential, of course, I kept asking myself, what does one do about examining ego and also one's self? Is self really ego? And vice versa? But why are self and ego so important to me now, but never seem to have troubled me in earlier life? I mean, after all, here in Macrobia, we're no longer competing in the work place for jobs, or maneuvering politically for a coveted position in some organization, craving recognition from superiors or fellow workers. None of us is requesting raises, yearning for promotions, or seeking peer relationships. We're all, most of us at least in this the third half of our lives, supposed to have retired from handling those sorts of pressures. For sure, aren't we relieved from such stressful hassles? No longer do we have careers on our mind to pursue until our retirement closes out that phase of our lives. In Macrobia, we have arrived at the culmination of our long career tunnel. There are no jobs to interview for, no pressure on us, or are there? Or are the pressures drawn on a different canvas with new colors unique to retirement, unique to this place? Yes, I believe that is so.

I posed the question to Walter: "In Macrobia, aren't we each seeking some degree of recognition, and in so doing wanting the respect of others? To achieve these goals, doesn't one need to tout their own past careers with all their accomplishments, hide behind the protective armor of our own egos and, in so doing, promote our own selves—such efforts being required here in order to make and keep Macrobia friends?"

Walter came back with, "Is that the right way to look at things?"

"Well, while attending events, I observe that everyone is, how shall I say, blowing their own horn."

"Doing what?"

"Touting their careers, their families, the size of their homes in Macrobia, their new furniture, their new car, their latest cruise ship journey. Going on in their self-promotion, some tout the many scholastic and/or career accomplishments of their children and grandchildren. Many engage in a mock contest by reciting a count of how many continents on earth they have visited, moving right up there to reach the total number visited to include each of the 8 continents. They would recite dates their cruise ships took them to each continent, concluding with number 8 being Antarctica. It is if they were challenging all around them to, "Top that if you can!" But that couple was taken aback when one person spoke up to say they'd been close to the North Pole—and isn't that a continent, too?—for they had recently sailed through the Northwest Passage, where they'd photographed polar bears at play on ice floats… see my pictures. Aren't the cubs cute?"

I clenched my fists, hit the table hard and exploded to Walter, "Living here in Macrobia you've got to compete! Right? Or else you're relegated to that invisible status where, when you want to talk to someone, their attention turns to another who is extolling their accomplishments. So, they've turned away and are now talking to that someone else, or else they're not listening to you, or they are over-talking you, going on about themselves, all the while boosting, at least in their own mind, their status."

Walter shrugged his shoulders. "So?"

I was growing edged with the subject, with myself, and with Walter. I thought more about my experiences in this retirement community and wanted to try to express myself to my friend. "Look, Walter, our fellow residents for the most part have come from homogeneous life patterns, more-or-less normal marriages, careers in Capitalist corridors, or in government jurisdictions, in non-profits, or maybe even family businesses."

I got a nod and so I went on, "Whereas today the young people I've read about can each come from a multiplicity of backgrounds, be they ethnic, or spiritual, and certainly geographical, much more so than us elders. Unlike our backgrounds, these young people appear to admire the diversity of life that surrounds each of them today."

"Do you mean young people are more open minded?"

I nodded at my friend. "Yes, it seems that way to me." I thought more and added, "They appear less resistant to change, for after all, technology is changing so fast one dare not resist the daily developments, or else one wakes up to yesterday." I tried to hum a tune, but was no good at it, and so I went on to evoke a memory of a song, "Yes, 'Here Come the Young!'" I told Walter I remembered that tune from years ago when the Baby Boomers were massing on the border of life intent on invading society and taking it over, which they promptly did. "Same thing today," I proffered, adding, "Except the young are younger and the old are older, and I'm among the older. Me and you—my friend Walter, the two us living here in Macrobia."

CHAPTER 9
THE OLD STAGECOACH STOP

I have a very acute sense of place and time,
so all my stories are rooted in a place and time
—*Isabel Allende*

The other night, Walter and I were talking as we sat in a corner of the little bar in Macrobia's historic stage stop. This cozy antique venue serves as an ideal setting for expressing confidential inter-personal revelations.

In earlier times, the stage stop, which is now listed on the National Register of Historic Places, was on the oft-traveled stage route that passed through this part of the state. That was back when this land was part of Mexico. According to the bronze plaque that extols the stage stop's heritage that is affixed to the wall outside the entry door, in 1846 Senor Ramon Gonzalez, exploiting his rumored connections in Mexico City, received a Mexican Land Grant covering most of the land in these parts, including what has become Macrobia. On his brown-sheeted *diseno*, or deed, Gonzalez's land was called the Gonzalez Ranchero. Its boundaries were delineated by black lines that also detailed lakes, bays, mountains, and rivers. Gonzalez himself, with a mind to the future, had posted the official parchment above the bar for everyone, including us retired folks today, to see and admire as his record of land grant ownership. As you set foot on the stone entry steps and entered the old coach stop, your attention immediately focused on the document, and you felt as if you were about to explore a chapter of California history.

In those days, Senior Gonzalez made the stop into a tavern serving food and drink for travelers, as for himself the old barn that stood outback being for the horses. Later, after the railroads came and stagecoaches were relegated to the past, the old place continued as his home. The large carved mahogany bar remained, its implied memories and its sense of importance giving Gonzalez and those who were his friends and business partners a sense of his cherished heritage. For us Macrobians, this sense of place linked us to the past, a past even more vintage that we.

That evening Walter had commented to me that Gonzales' story wasn't so unusual. "There were Mexican Land Grants on most of the land around Macrobia throughout the state." He explained further, "That was back before the area became part of the United States under the protection of General Kearney and his advancing Army of the West that, having marched all the way to Monterey, triggered the Treaty of Guadalupe-Hidalgo ending the Mexican War."

I was reminded that today most of us living in this community feel well protected, for ours is a gated community. Once in, you're in, not for good, well, yes, pretty much for good, allowing for occasional outside trips to Trader Joes, the theater, and one of the three international airports close by, by taxi, by train, or by car when you want to or need to just go bye-bye, only to be required by the limiting constraints of age to return, sooner or later.

*   *   *

As I said, I think Walter is about a year older. Shows, too. He walks with his special cane whose ivory tip unscrews. Inside, in the hollow interior, so he once showed me, is a scroll detailing his final documents. It is tied with a black bow and, so he said, includes his living trust, a final will in case he's on the gurney and lost his senses, a power of attorney to his son in some place called Drain, Oregon, and a sheet of his most valuable postage stamps.

He untied the bow and unfurled the sheet of stamps for me that evening, expecting me to admire them, one by one, which I did, of course. This part of his unique stamp collection was from Epirus. He told me he'd once been there and explored the medieval town of Gyrokaster. By the time he was there, Epirus was no more and that town was in Albania—back when Enver Hoxha was in charge of that communist and atheist country. That bit of data, I suppose, was intended to impress me. Well, it did, because I knew from my collection of Albanian postage stamps that no one ever got in or went out of Albania on their own while Enver was running things. Maybe running is a grade too high. Better, while he was pouring concrete for his absurd pillboxes, which he spotted all around the little country. Inside them, his soldiers would be told to crouch, there prepared to shoot the Americans when the imperialist capitalist Nord Amerikanskis invaded—an event he told them was imminent. That was back when we lived under the cloud of the Cold War. Albania, of course, still exists, and I have a set of Albanian stamps with Enver's dictatorial picture.

I'll concede that Walter had been to that medieval town of Gyrokaster. Friends don't pick apart friends stories, do they? Well, the Epirus stamps are Walter's focal point in his strange collection. He had already explained that he collects philatelic history from countries like Epirus, explaining to me that it was a breakaway from Greece in what was then the Turkish Ottoman Empire. Walter explained that in that day's game of thrones, half of Epirus wound up in what is now Albania, the balance in Greece.

The next evening in his home, he retrieved two 78-rpm records and played them, one by one, on his retro turntable, explaining during breaks in the music, that they were Epriotic folk music from the 1920s and 30s. "Quite rare, and very inspiring, don't you think?" he said briefly, as I smiled in support of my friend's interests and especially his research. For emphasis, and to my amazement, he added, "Some say it is Europe's oldest folk music."

Without chagrin, Walter reminded me that briefly existing countries such as Epirus reminded him of himself. Over time, in a series of reminisces, he confided that he had been in a couple of marriages, more than one or two small business as an entrepreneur, and once was a traveling vagabond, without a thing to worry about. He also recited, when at a young age, he was briefly enrolled in a seminary program in order to avoid the draft during the Korean War. That stint was brief and, he confided, a big disappointment, for the seminary did not offer studies in the host of Eastern religions or beliefs.

By that time in his life, Walter said, he found himself flirting with Buddhism. In the Christian seminary, such devious behavior of spiritual exploration was forbidden. The novitiates dared not veer from the prescribed beliefs. Interest in Hinduism, Buddhism, Zoroaster, or any of the other Eastern religions or spiritual quests was cause for dismissal, which the fathers, or was it the abbot, having found out, promptly did to my curious friend Walter.

The seminary, he told me, for he had gone back years later to hand out Buddhist literature, was still there, but under a different name, studying a different religion, the grounds adorned with different statues, all being attended to by a host of novitiates. He was surprised to find young men intent on their studies, because the Korean and Viet Nam military draft had finally ended, along with the need for deferments.

His experience with religion, Walter told me, was just like these countries whose stamps he collected, for like them, the land, the people, and the culture were probably still there but under another name, another ruler, another belief ritual and dogma, even though the indigenous culture continued to persist. And he, Walter, was still extant, still eschewing breakaway spiritual beliefs in pursuit of his own insatiable exploratory curiosity.

The flags of those countries, whose stamps Walter collected, in effect—at least for him—unfurled unique banners of political and cultural designs. The result was that his personal flag was now of a different sort. And those no-longer-used postage stamps had come to form his stamp collection. He smiled over a few of the Epirus stamps, including the colorful one with their flag. Therein lay the stamps' value, and maybe each of our own residual values, as well, as we salute our own personal flag. At least it seemed that way in Walter's world. To me, Walter seemed to be excelling, happy in his life in Macrobia,

In telling me these things, he periodically laughed heartily, as old men like Walter, and me, can do and do well. Yet to me, like many of the men here, he was a strange sort of fellow… maybe unique would be a more appropriate description. Yes, I'll use that adjective. Walter, my close friend, and I his.

CHAPTER 10
GENDER ROLES

A gender-equal society would be one where the word 'gender'
does not exist: where everyone can be themselves.
—Gloria Steinem

Walter recounted to me that, from time to time in his life, he had undertaken a panoply of pursuits, both entrepreneurial while several times trying to work for others. Like his stamps from countries that also didn't make it, Walter was seldom successful with any of his endeavors. Perhaps verbally intruding, I asked him how he was able to get the money to move into Macrobia. I mean, your FICO score was pulled off the Internet and your credit report was examined. Your income was analyzed. These examinations took place after you'd demonstrated that you had either the cash to buy a place, or else qualified for a home loan. In response to my conern, he advised, "All it takes is one windfall."

Along with others, male and female, I had made it through the labyrinth of vetting in order to qualify to live here. During this process, there was no gender difference. Yet what did bother me, I finally admitted, were the gender roles assigned to those of us, male and female, making up the members of our generation. We had each grown up helpless as we dutifully followed these precisely defined gender roles, having been offered no acceptable alternative in our life assignments.

That is, until quite recently, when today's gender identity began to change as we advanced into the 21st century. These new developments, of course, came not in time to alter or adjust the gender positions we were required to play in our earlier stages of life, given the scripts dealt to us, which, as young men and young women, we were instructed to read, memorize, and to go forth and enact.

You might argue, as Walter did with me, that the earlier scenario had played itself out by now, but I disagreed with him, saying it had not. I expounded, "Our generation's male roles fell along prescribed lines: there was the duty of us males to find a job so we could provide for our family. In those days, we were all on stage in the same decades, acting in comparable scenes and similar roles. In these separate but more or less identical scripts, with carbon copy stage instructions handed to each of us, we males had the responsibility of bringing home the income. Plus, in anticipation of our actuarial death, which would surely occur prior to the wife's, we were charged, through our last wills and testaments, with providing one of several types of trusts, assuring financial wellbeing for the wife and family. That had been the rulebook for the game of life in my generation and the ones before me and to some extent the ones following me."

Walter acknowledged it had been for him, as well, although he hadn't followed it faithfully. He said, "Yes, we were all recruited by the same life coach and played in the same league of life, and were judged by the same set of umpires and referees, be they religious or judicial."

CHAPTER 11
WHAT MAKES MALE SUCCESS?

To travel hopefully is a better thing than to arrive,
and the true success is to labour.
—*Robert Louis Stevenson*

In Walter's philosophy of his stamp collecting, financially at least, once in a while a country did work—perhaps one of his failed countries was acquired by another country, absorbed, its folks integrated. So, had it been that way with Walter? Perhaps one or two of his business endeavors had been acquired by another, larger, more successful corporation. In their buyout or his sellout, Walter had reaped his monetary harvest, like a lottery ticket paying off.

"All it takes is one," he repeated to me as he recounted his panoply of careers and endeavors. "Even in failure, there are rewards," he pontificated. "Take the Confederacy," he said, "it didn't evaporate. Its lands, its soil, its people have been incorporated into the Union. Many cities have become major automobile and parts manufacturers, and their colleges excel, don't they?"

Of course, I had to agree—not that I debated the question, for I knew, as did everyone, that Old Dixie was not today a wasteland, unpopulated, unfarmed, and as forlorn as the Moon is reported to be. If their country folded, it did come back, and in the same way, could people who suffered reverses, even sought counseling in troubled situations, or maybe didn't, but nevertheless had come back, re-entering the playing fields of life.

My curiosity about Walter extended, of course, to his earlier life, going before enterprise, to his family. I assumed he had one—most everyone living here did, in varying sizes, shapes, and degrees of affection. I inquired. Walter replied, saying little other than to tell one story, albeit succinctly, about one wife, only to revert back to talking about his stamps by telling another story—always to me interesting, so I listened politely and even intently—about how he had assembled his rather extensive and quite specialized collection of postage stamps.

Still, I thought I'd try once again to probe more about his background.

CHAPTER 12
A CONFRONTATION

We should look long and carefully at ourselves
before we pass judgment on others.
—Molierer

N ot everything in Macrobia is picture perfect, whatever a new
arrival's anticipation might suggest. So far, during my life
here, I've met a dozen or so men. Of them, maybe three
might be considered sort-of friends, ones with whom I have an
occasional conversation. But Walter is my best friend. The others are
sort-ofs, where we say hello to each other, maybe talk about a sports
event, a political crises somewhere in the world, and then wish each
other a nice day, before parting. Surface banter. But it is a tad more
intimate than the occasional few words with the women I happen to
encounter. I mean, I find on many days I have more to talk about
with the friendly checker at the local Trader Joe's.

Summing up as a single male, it's lonely here. There are all these
people walking about, driving their cars, new and not so new,
participating in one club event after the other. It's not like you're in
solitary, although you might as well be, given the lack of desired talk
therapy—that is, of the wished-for vital conversations—the deeper
than surface back and forth, from which you ideally would benefit in
trying to navigate the days, weeks, and months of being in this place.
Perhaps because we males are supposed to act like mates, we are
expected to repeat our unique individual accomplishments each time
we see each other, or so I related to Walter. He nodded agreement,
recalling, I'm sure, his own intra-male episodes.

But then, as I related to Walter, "Came an unwelcome and

unexpected negative experience. I am trying to sort it out, you might say, to try to recover from the episode. At least, it seems to always be on my mind, troubling me." I went on, explaining to Walter, "You see, in my outreach to meet other men, I thought I had found a friend in a guy named Champ. He and I enjoyed similar interests. As a retired member of the clergy, Champ had become the esteemed president of a political club, in the process and over time becoming an icon. He was about the only male member of the club, so I came to find out. I joined the club and received a perfunctory nod from him and a welcome wave and smile from Rose, the female club vice-president."

Walter seemed a little bored, but I continued anyway, "At the next club event, he saw me talking to Rose. Ours was a brief conversation about the political state of national affairs. Apparently, he perceived my familiarity with her to be an act threatening his role as the club's male leader presiding over his loyal female congregation. He began to gaslight me, advising the club board that I was handicapped with a dour personality. Even more worrisome, having learned from our conversations that I had been in therapy, which I had been years ago after my wife's passing. How he found out, I don't know, but he told many of the club members, as such, I was a dangerous person to be allowed in their midst."

Walter supplied my conclusion, "And, as everyone in the know knows, a person in therapy offers a warning. After all, something must be wrong up there, else why would they be in therapy? We normals are not in therapy, and we're okay! Aren't we?" But then Walter looked hard at me and challenged, "But you don't really know all this, Jerry, about Champ. You're surmising a lot."

I thought Water might be right, but then I recited my anger toward Champ. "What right does he have," I asked Walter, "to put me down? After all, we're living in this retirement community, accommodating our aging together, sharing our problems, hopefully with compassion for each other, aren't I right about that?"

Walter held up his hand, "Forget it," he advised. He went on, "Look, Jerry, each of us old folks here in Macrobia have had long lives. We've surely learned a lot of things. And one thing is that we've got to get beyond judging other people. Few of us are credentialed to do that. And when it come to pass that you're being judged by someone, simply overlook it, ignore the affront, go on with your life, and…"

"…And?"

"Jerry, forget it. Ignore this old preacher. Stay away from him." Walter held up his hand and said strongly, "Put this unfortunate incident behind you. Even if what you say is true, so what?" He softened, taking a little pity on me, I felt, and went on to describe his take on many of the men he'd come across here in Macrobia. "Some of these guys, Jerry, can't shift gears and allow themselves to enter into retirement, so I've come to conclude. They are still trapped in the confining world of male competition, one against another. Your Champ is apparently locked in that judgmental category. Have compassion for him, for he is lagging the pack here in Macrobia. In my opinion, we each need to feel and express to everyone a certain camaraderie of aging. We need to help each other, be supportive of one another."

Walter encouraged me to read more about Buddhism and practice meditation, explaining to me more about this discipline, aspects of which I'd never heard. Well, there are lots of things I've never heard of, I can tell you that for free right now. But the concept, as related by Water, caused me, with his direction and encouragement, to explore Buddhism by pursuing my own regimen of daily meditation.

"It is not a traditional top-down voice from a higher authority, which is the practice of organized religious dogma," Walter explained. "The Buddhist philosophy of life, in order for it to work for you, must come from within."

CHAPTER 13
FAMILY DAY AT THE POOL

When but a little boy, it seemed
My dearest rapture ran
In fancy ever, when I dreamed
I was a man—a man!
Now—sad perversity—my theme
Of rarest, purest joy
Is when, in fancy blest, I dream
I am a little boy.
—James Whitcomb Riley

During Festivities Week, this one day was being celebrated as "American Family Day." Walter and I were lounging in deck chairs at the picnic area next to the largest of the community's swimming pools. There were lots of little boys and girls in the water and playing on the manicured green grass hugging the edges of the pool. Picnic tables were filled with food. Little coolers with ice and drinks were watched over by attentive grandparents and parents, everyone relishing in the day's family camaraderie.

"Remember when?" Walter asked, gesturing at the little children of both genders and of all sizes romping about. "Seems like just yesterday."

"No it doesn't, Walter. It was decades ago, not yesterday."

"You're older."

"No, you are."

We let it go at that. But not really. The subject hung over my emotions for a while, and then I instructed myself to let it go. Families with little children were experiences from yesteryear, a bygone era for me and I suspected for Walter. Memories lingered, mine, and I presume Walter's, too. Some of mine were painful. Others, especially those with Matilda, were pleasant. Reluctantly, and really beyond my emotional control, I visited them because they were there, and when memories are in your mind, on your screen, in your heart, you can't delete them; there's no app for that. I suppose it was that way for Walter.

Trying to shift my mind onto a different wavelength, I recalled noticing that women get to know other women by asking questions about their children. Women, so I had concluded, were more oriented to children, since they were the gender that had them, and that made sense to me as we sat by the pool observing the little ones. So, I asked Walter to tell me more about his children.

"The Six," he said as he retrieved an aberrant beach ball and, smiling, tossed it the short distance to a toddler with her welcoming arms outstretched. "There you are," he said to the tyke, softly. Walter had obviously executed that ball-throwing maneuver many times those years ago. I sensed he relished doing it again this day.

He looked at me in earnest and repeated his children count. "Yes, and each had their own first day of issue. That's when they are fresh from the engraver, uncancelled… pristine… my mint block of six— in full color. Their portraits adorn my own personal stamp collection." He smiled, proudly I thought, and went on, "In their case, I have an album showing their country and their characters, each still in existence."

"Your ongoing interests," I suggested, and he nodded. Yet I could see he had reservations, for his nod was brief and replaced with a furrowing of his brow before he tossed the conversational ball to me, asking, "And about yours?"

I troubled how I might reply. Estranged? Or in contact with? I wanted to ask, to clarify, but didn't. Keep it simple, I instructed myself. "My three?" I heard myself say, followed by my silence. Then I thought to ask, "Where? I mean, where are your six now? Nearby? Do you see them often? Do they visit you here, or you there, wherever there is?"

Another beach ball bounded our way, the retrieval delaying

Walter's answer. This time I returned the big ball to a little girl who smiled back, sweetly. I choked up. How long had it been? Had I taken the time, exerted the effort to mentally calculate, I would know the answer, gnawing on me as it might. Memories went back, and back. Memories are like files in a filing cabinet, there when you want them, because one has no problem opening the right drawer. But then comes the process of extracting the file folder. Peering in causes the eruption of emotions, the tear perhaps, the joy hopefully, the re-play of visions, the candid camera shots filed away in one's own mental album with the remembrances from one's personal iPhoto application. I said for some reason, factually wanting Walter to know, or else just reminding myself, "Yes, two boys and a girl."

"Five girls and a boy," came his statement. "Scattered," he added, "in as many countries." He shook his head, suggesting to me he didn't understand their motives, their objectives in life. He appended with, "On three continents."

I suggested, "Great opportunities to collect stamps."

He lamented, "They don't write; don't post mail; instead, once in a while, one of them tweets. Email is old fashioned, one of them told me." He shrugged, "I guess, while you, Jerry, and I have ageing within our life's familiar confines, life elsewhere in the world has moved on." In a philosophical tone that Walter displayed on rare occasions such as this one, he asked himself and me, "What sort of persons do they think their own kids are going to grow into? I mean, growing up in a foreign country that is not their native culture, where few speak their native language." Walter despaired, as if he required me to answer, but then added, "How are our grandkids going to make it in life?"

I felt compassion for him. Slowly I asked, "How many grandkids?"

"Five," he said promptly, but then hesitated, and I thought he smiled in a proud sort of way. Then, without warning, he blurted, "Let's get a beer." It was uncharacteristic of Walter, for he seldom said anything so sharply different from our conversation at the time. His beverage request arrived from out of the blue.

*   *   *

Retreat to the Stage Stop

"Family Day at the Pool" having been left behind, as we walked, I imagined the cool air inside our historic stagecoach pub. There, I reasoned, it might be easier to talk about his, and then my kids, and the subject that was sure to follow—their mothers, our wives, our grieving, at least mine. I didn't know about Walter's.

So, the two of us old guys walked over to the old stagecoach stop, without a coach and horses, as I like to picture the place all those years ago. Once there, each of us was destined to talk about things occurring to us not all those many years ago.

Walter and I ensconced ourselves in a corner table. The walls behind us were decorated with horsey things and an old folk oil painting of the stagecoach stop in the days of yesteryear, showing a stage with its horses hitched. Baggage sat on the rack appended to the rear of the coach. Two bearded rough-looking guys in typical western attire hoisting shotguns sat astride the plank seat. With his other hand, one gripped the reins that would control and direct the team of four powerful and magnificent horses.

As I began to down the draft, I saw the stage's packed-away baggage. Suddenly I welcomed the opportunity for my personal baggage to be unloaded. It had been too long since I had exposed my mental belongings. I went first. As I did, I detected a sign of relief on Walter's face that he was momentarily freed from revealing his deep personal history to me.

I heard myself say, "Now, in the third half of my life—"

Walter interrupted, "Jerry, you can't have three halves in a whole. You can only have two halves—"

I shot back, "Look, Walter, it's my life, I can have—"

"—Okay, okay, between us, in your life you can have however many halves you want. So, tell me about your wife, the mother, so I presume, of your three kids." He motioned my way. "You're on, my friend."

Of course, I knew the math about halves, but it was the most appropriate way for me to describe my life, so I went on, "The first half went from age zero to 20-plus, or thereabouts. It was life through schooling—basic, then elementary—followed by years at college. The second half extended through my job—years of a career, or in my case a start at a career and then a life change to my permanent and long-lasting career—"

"—Thought you said you had only one career."

"Right… I did, but that wasn't right."

"It was wrong!"

"Right."

Walter looked at me, waiting, his eyes and expression urging me on.

"But the third half of my life has come along later—now here in Macrobia. It began with the events that propelled me to this place. Today I am living the third half of my life!"

Walter urged, "So, tell me about each… well, I pretty well know the third half, right?"

"Right." I sipped the brew and went on, "Life number two began with the Korean War…"

"The draft."

"Right." I fell silent, but soon elaborated, "It was also the Cold War with the looming threat of World War III and Soviet atomic bombs waiting in silos in Siberia to be launched our way."

Walter acknowledged, "There was talk of war all around us."

I nodded. "I met this young woman. We dated. We… at least I… fell in love. It was the height of uncertain times. The world as we knew It might end in a billowing series of mushroom clouds."

Walter nodded knowingly.

"I was in college courtesy of a deferment. Somehow, the people running the country in those days valued a college education above shooting guns or dropping atomic bombs. Of course, I agreed with them."

"So you got married?"

"Well, sort of."

"Now, what the hell does that mean?"

"Just what I said." Silence, but soon I continued, "We had a kid, a baby, an offspring."

"Got it! Go on."

"I told the military I was a father."

"Well, you were."

Again, I nodded. "So, my deferment held for a bit. But—"

"But?"

"It lapsed. Maybe they found out I wasn't, you know, formally married. I was re-classified 1-A, or was it A-1? Anyway, by then I had become determined I wasn't going to leave my body and my hopes on some wretched blood-soaked, ice-crusted Korean battlefield halfway around the world, lying there in sub-zero weather, a victim of some nameless Chinese bullet from a nameless Chinese machine gun fired by some nameless poor Chinese soldier imported into North Korea to shoot and kill Americans on some damn peninsula appended to the vast Asian continent, whose language I couldn't speak, and whose history I knew little about."

Walter opined, "Or even cared about, at least at that time in your life." He quickly added, "I think I know what's coming."

"Yeah, you got it, Walter."

"How long were you in Canada?"

"Long enough to enroll in the University of Toronto and eventually get my degree in history of the western world from the Renaissance on up to what was then the present time."

"And your young woman and kid?"

"I left a little girl… and her baby… in New York Town, per Harry Belafonte."

"Regrets?"

"You bet. As had all those soldiers, some of whom I knew—buddies in high school from my neighborhood. They did their duty and died on that damned Korean peninsula. Some of their remains remain there."

Walter pressed, "How did your family—mother and father—react to your going to Canada to avoid the draft and being sent to Korea?"

"They were humiliated. They unfriended me, as young people say today. I was disgraced among the family and the friends of theirs who always flew the flag, even on days that weren't flag days. My father, well… he shot himself."

Walter stumbled out, "I'm sorry to hear that."

I added, to complete the story, "And then my mother went into a rehab facility, but never rehabbed."

"Feelings of guilt? You? I mean."

"Me? Sure. To this day." By now, my mug of beer was consumed. I looked Walter in the eye and said emphatically, "But why doesn't someone tell the world about the diplomats who, after World War II, allowed the Korean Peninsula to be divided along that artificial geographic parallel line? And then there were our diplomats who said the South wasn't within our—the U.S.'s—sphere of influence, thus inviting the North to invade the South. And then there were the military generals and admirals who weren't prepared. And what about the air force that in 1950 when the war started was still flying propeller airplanes from vintage World War II when the North Koreas had their jet planes and their tanks from Russia when they crossed that parallel line and attacked the South? And then where were the intelligence services that didn't alert the generals about the North's military buildup. Or alert them about the Chinese soldiers swarming across the Yalu River to fight our boys? I could go on and on and on."

After that exchange, Walter and I sat in silence, neither knowing what to say. Soon Walter grasped my arm and squeezed it several times. Melting, I cried.

I wiped my eyes, looked at Walter and said, "I've always thought about writing down my feelings, my thoughts, my actions." I admitted to myself that I had always wanted to underline my thoughts. I mean, I had always admired Matilda and her skills in writing her columns. I did think my thoughts were valid. But for me to share them with strangers? To set them out in a form of writing that others could see? No way, but yet maybe there is a way, along with my anti-war platform.

Walter suggested, "Now Jerry, here in Macrobia, you have the opportunity and the time to do so—to write your thoughts. Right?"

I took in Walter's suggestions and thought more about my experiences and how I might put them into some sort of writing expression. I allowed, "Well, my late wife Matilda was a writer—

maybe I didn't tell you that—so I suppose I could try."

"Look, Jerry, you might as well. Otherwise, no one else will ever have the opportunity to experience your experiences."

"But what if I don't write well, don't express myself well, don't—"

"—Stop with the don'ts," Walter admonished. He went on to relate his research experiences when he was looking into the story of one of his failed countries and their stamps. Then he said, "No telling what you will discover within yourself, as well as on the Internet and especially in the libraries when you start into a writing project. And, remember, if it doesn't work for you, and you give it up, you won't be any worse off than my friends in Epirus or the Confederacy, or—"

"—Stop with the failed countries."

"Then start with your writing." Walter added, "Go for it."

Friends, I thought, are for encouragement. "Yes," I said, telling him I would do it. In the days after that, I tried to organize a plan, an approach, an outline perhaps as to how I might go about pursuing this new literary venture of mine.

That was when I transported myself back in time to that one evening with Walter when he needed to stop telling me about the items occupying his shelves, for he said he must search his kitchen drawers for the corkscrew needed to open his pinot noir. There weren't that many drawers, so, "Surely it's here somewhere," he mumbled in frustration.

In my mind, searching for the corkscrew represented the same dilemma as prying around trying to understand Walter, or to devise a plan for my writing. Surely the corkscrew, or my thoughts, along with Walter's personal story, are both located somewhere. With each having been hopefully found, I would be itching to ask Walter for an explanation of his life, and why he pursued such a strange stamp collection. But, no, my finding out, along with my writing ideas, had to wait for the discovery of the damn corkscrew's hiding place. Actually, in my little place, I have two wine openers, just in case.

Walter had two deluxe crystal wine glasses ready for us. He clinked them and the lovely sound floated along his shelves and reverberated through his one bedroom with the tintinnabulation of musical accomplishment. I thought it was a sonorous endorsement of his living space, his mind, his shelves, but not his hiding corkscrew or even of him, himself. And I thought more about my nascent writing ideas.

CHAPTER 14
FAMILY

"...more unhappiness comes from this source than from any other—I mean from the attempt to prolong family connection unduly and to make people hang together artificially who would never naturally do so..."
—Samuel Butler

I thought more about my own family. Later, I said to Walter, going on and on as friends are permitted to do, "I once tried to get the family together for a reunion. It was for family's sake. And, of course, for my sake, and for the memory of Matilda, to whom I sensed a responsibility to her to report my efforts and the result—the hoped-for gathering of her family, and mine, to which I could somehow tell her about the event... sometime... when of course I knew that precious time with her could never happen. But then of course, I wished it might, so for my sake and the family's sake and her sake I tried for the reunion, and I tried hard. I made a major effort to get them all, each of them, to come together in a venue in what was my family's original hometown. There, I reasoned, surroundings would be familiar, both to them and to me. Their times past. Their times present. After all, she—my late wife, that is—gave birth to them, each of them one at a time, years apart, years ago when she was healthy, vibrant, caring, loving, and enduring the pain of childbirth—they don't remember. I asked myself if they cared—"

"—Did you ever care, Jerry, when you were that age?" Walter interrupted my diatribe. "I mean, that age when you had grown past being really young and were old enough to know, to reason, and as a result, to care?"

I stopped short. I thought. Slowly I answered, "No," adding, of course, "I see your point." Yet I didn't, but I felt I should say, "You're right, Walter." And then I asked, "Is it the same with you?"

Walter nodded.

I thought he wanted me to go on about my family. "Want to know what happened?" But I wondered, with so many of the years having passed by and so quickly disappearing into years later, did I really no longer care what happened at that traditional American family get together of mine? Of course I did, I assured myself. So, I told Walter, "In preparation for their visit, and I hoped they would each come, I rented the conference room in the restaurant we all used to go to as a family, well, once or twice, I suppose, as I think back. Not like a generational hangout. Not like in the Old Country. There, families stay together from one generation to the next, don't wander off. They meet in the same place year after year. Thinking about the matter, I was reminded that here, in the good old US of A... we live in a culture where, instead, families fly apart... disperse... even worldwide."

Walter interjected, "Families think they're still printing their own collectible postage stamps, hoping they will be like the ones you, Jerry, collect, not the out-of-existence ones I collect."

Why Walter said that troubled me momentarily, but then he urged me to continue my story, which I did, saying, "Two of my three showed up—the guys with their wives, well, one was his fiancé, the other his at-the-time—what do you say? companion? Girl friend? Anyway, the two of them. The daughter didn't show or didn't call, or didn't email until days later, only then asking if she had missed something."

"Crass," Walter intoned.

I was too upset to react with a reply, but after a few minutes, I did, saying, "I told her we had a nice family reunion without she and her by-then husband." I hesitated. Then I had to say it, but I regretted mouthing the words, yet what I was about to say was "on topic," that being living with age, which covers, for sure, the attributes of age. "Walter," I began, as he waved his hand in a circular motion, his signal for me to continue, "why are our young offspring—our kids and their spouses, if they've got any, or their—what are they called these days?"

"Significant others."

I nodded at the term and went on, "Why don't they acknowledge the effects age is having on us—their parents?"

Walter said, "You know, Jerry, I've been wondering the same thing. With the little contact I have with my six and their others, when I do, they think I can walk as fast as they can, flit about like they do, jump around as if they and I were six years old, but I'm eighty years beyond that level of energy and dexterity, Jerry. There's no recognition on their part of the age difference between them and me. Nor are they aware of any of the impairments that advancing age delivers." He looked hurt and added, "Nor do they seem to care. These matters are simply not on their cell phone screens or sounding from their always-present high-tech earphones."

I asked, "But why not?" And then I thought more about family, my kids. None of my three, as far as I could recall, ever asked me about any accomplishments I may have had in my long life. Or the times I had been upset, maybe depressed, both of us, Matilda and me. I asked Walter the same question I'd just asked myself.

He thought for a while, his mind churning, and then replied, "Because children see their parents the same way we see an actor on the stage or on the silver screen. We all see the character they play, the image the actor becomes, not the person the actor is beneath their stage facade. If we were to sit down with that actor for a beer, we'd be mute, not knowing what to say to them as an individual person. We'd probably default to them as an actor, asking about a role they'd played, then defaulting back to silence."

"Same with family. In other words, you're saying we're an actor on their stage of life, not a real live person to get to know, to buddy with, as we used to say all those years ago, not like someone they're wanting to be friends with."

Walter nodded and then said, "I think it's because of the stereotypes the media—TV and what little they read on their cell phones—depict us old people to be like. In other words, each of us is a character actor on the TV or movie screen, or in a stage play and, for sure, not a person to get to know as a friend. So, our kids and other young people likely perceive us as fitting into one of these media stereotypes, such as being forgetful, pushing two canes or an awkward walker, or else trying to maneuver around in a motorized wheelchair."

"Walter, do they have any understanding of the fragility and apprehension that ride shotgun across our age stage?"

"What you're saying, Jerry, is that I could collapse any minute now with a stroke of some sort—possibly caused by an array of developing or sudden physical conditions in my aging body—an aneurism, a sudden defect in my circulation, a clot on my consciousness. Not likely, but any of these ailments could suddenly pop up and crash me to the floor." Walter looked sad, an expression he had not revealed before. He pined, "Do they even consider the devastation a stroke could befall upon either of us?"

Thinking more about strokes, I added, "Yes, a stroke could be that—the finale—if we didn't get the medics here for you or for me within the prescribed medical time frame."

Walter said, "Remember, Jerry, when we were kids and one of us got injured—maybe broke a bone sliding into second base in a Little League baseball game...."

"...Yeah."

"Well, there were lots of people with help, the coach, the parents in the stands, the other players. Off to the x-ray room at the ERA, maybe into the hospital, but certainly enough band aids and care swarming over."

"And now?"

"Now, you get a well-intentioned paramedic armed with a stereotypical view of the aged person, and a by-yourself ride to the emergency room in an ambulance with a quick follow-up bill that you hope will be covered by Medicare."

"Quite a difference age and time do make," I concluded, finding myself in sync with Walter's nod.

Mulling those words, we two old guys sat there in silence, not selling anything to each other. Perhaps that's one measure of male friendship—no intent on the part of either guy to sell the other anything. I suppose we were checking our tire pressures and heart beats and whatever else you can monitor when you are suddenly face to face with the overwhelming worries and concerns that ride piggyback on age, more specifically what can go wrong—at any moment. And, wow! What do I do? What do you do? And is this medical situation to be the last one I will ever experience in my end of life scenario now upon me?

Walter said, "Did I tell you about the woman acquaintance I've known from soon after my moving here?"

"No."

"She was backing her car out of her carport one morning, swim suit in her bag headed for one of the pools. When, all of a sudden... I mean, that was it. The car hit the embankment behind and stopped as she crumpled over the steering wheel. No warning. No goodbyes. No prayers. Nada. A neighbor saw it and called the medics, who came promptly—within minutes, but to no avail."

Again, we sat in silence, perhaps in tribute, perhaps glad; no, not glad, thankful maybe that it wasn't either of us, but realizing that at any time, at any day, at any hour it could have been either of us—that is, if the gods of life governance frowned upon either of us. Those gods didn't need a reason, an excuse, a prod—they just did their thing, dropping down their final curtain on one of life's terminated players.

I said, "Back home, a friend of mind—owned a prestigious art gallery—a pillar of the community—was driving his car when the end came. His car went into the storm ditch alongside the road, his lifeless body pinched between the steering wheel and the deployed air bag. I had often seen him running along the same street with his Dalmatian. We had always waved."

"Yeah, and what happens if I have a stroke?"

"You get no warning."

"That's it. It just comes. Out of the blue. Zap. You've been hit, like a lightning bolt from nowhere.

"No one cares," I suggested. "No member of my family, I mean. Neighbors and friends, if you've got any, probably care more than family." I paused. "Geez, did I say that?"

"You did, but if you hadn't I would have." Thoughtfully, Walter went on, "Friends are important in many situations, replacing family members." Walter held up his hand, his palm pointing at me. I braced myself, as I felt something of even more import was coming. It did. He said, "You know what your problem is, Jerry?"

I said, "No, but I'm sure I'd benefit from knowing, especially with its dimensions coming from you."

Ignoring my remark, Walter said, "You—and maybe me, too—try to address today's living, and I mean in this place, by relying on judgments and outlooks learned three-quarters of a century ago. While that wisdom and, if you will call it such, represents the street smarts of yesteryear, well, those tidbits of wisdom just don't apply today. Oh, maybe some do, like be nice to people, love one another, and all that, but as far as understanding behavior of our kids and others here in Macrobia, forget it, for the world marches to different tunes today than when you and I were kids growing up. In those times, we were job seekers looking for work, and maybe getting it and trying to adjust to the adult world."

"Are you saying my outlook on family does not reflect the values I thought it might?"

"Yes."

"And?"

Walter asked, "Did you grow up with a religion, a church, or whatever, that you went to, maybe with your parents?"

I nodded. "Yes, for a while. I mean, until I went away to college."

"What happened then?"

I thought back and told my friend, "I came home for the holidays, and my pastor asked me about my college experience. I related that one of my professors had asked if Jesus really did, ever, at any time, actually exist. So, I asked my pastor, who was a learned man of theological thought who had delivered Sunday sermons that were well researched and well thought out, usually conveying an inspirational message."

"How did he react to your inquisitive nature?"

"He bristled, turned crimson in his holy face and told me that I should simply follow what my elders told me—meaning him—about Jesus and quit delving into areas in which I was not academically trained."

"How'd you feel about that?"

"About how I feel about you telling me that how we approached life back then may not work today. I'm devastated, but curious. And I'll tell you what I've done all my life after that incident."

"And that is?"

"I've nurtured my curiosity and struggled to explore the culture we find ourselves in… maybe adrift in, especially in Macrobia."

"Here?"

"Like here, when you told me what my problem is. Now I realize I've more paths to explore and terrain to travel if I'm going to make progress in this, the third half of my life."

"Jerry, that's the benefit you and I now have with this old age of yours and mine. As have so many other folks living here, we've been given time. It's like we've hit the double 'O' on the roulette wheel of life. Now we have the chance to gather in our winning chips and the opportunity to spend our winnings."

"Before someone else spins our giant wheel of life with a different result."

Walter nodded. "Take advantage of our winnings. Our time is here today. The time for saving is past. Now's the time to spend and benefit. Yield to the present."

I mused and commented, "So long as we don't run out of chips."

"Then what would we do, each of us?"

I didn't know, and I didn't want to go there, even if hypothetical. My voice choking, I suggested, "There's always the homeless, sleeping bags and tents. Under the big fig tree in Santa Barbara, or in the shelter offered on the concrete sidewalk outside the Symphony Hall."

Walter said softly, "Those poor guys."

In silence, I nodded.

*   *   *

A Reunion

Later I said to Walter, "Do you know what one of my sons said to me right after he arrived for our family reunion? I mean, maybe five minutes after our perfunctory handshakes and the obligatory arms-outstretched hug?"

Walter thought. "You want me to guess, and maybe I'll win a prize for being right-on." Once more, he chuckled, but then promptly grew more serious. Walter knew the ensuing scenario or close to it, likely from his own experiences. Maybe this is why we're friends. We both have similar family experiences, one of the ingredients that make up the recipe for friendship.

I said, "We were standing there in the back of the restaurant. My son looked around. It was a plain room with a framed Rockwell painting of a family at Thanksgiving dinner with the father about to slice into the golden brown turkey, his carving knife and fork ready, alongside the cranberries and stuffing. There were eager faces, hungry faces, family faces. The Rockwell was hanging crookedly on the sidewall. My son blurted, 'Why did you choose this place? I mean, it's more fun to go to that pizza place out by the freeway—she and I— he gestured at his girlfriend, go there all the time. It jumps with background music. He went on, extolling the place called, 'Papa's Pizza.'"

I couldn't quote the rest of the conversation, but Walter knew the gist. He nodded while I tried to relate to him my take on the mental orientation of my son and my absent daughter. "In summary," I began—

—Walter interrupted, holding up his hand to stop me and, I presumed, ease my pain of having to continue with my story. Instead, my friend spoke in a soft confidential voice, as if he were sharing with me hidden generational secrets that had not been journalistically covered in the media, heard on TV, and certainly never brushed into a Rockwell painting. Walter told me, "I know. I've been there. Here's my take:"

I waited in anticipation. Memories of my failed family reunion— and I guess that's what we call them, reunions. If there's a union, how can there by a re-of one? The Union was the term used during the American Civil War. After the war there was not a re-Union. I thought of Walter's Confederate stamps, and I asked him about the use of the term. He advised that a reunion occurred when the "boys came home."

I allowed as how he was correct. But had that taken place in the South? "Because," I began, "You can only have a reunion if there is a place familiar to which you go or to which you 'come back to,' right? In the South there was only devastation. You could have a 'coming back', but not a 'reunion'."

Walter shook his head. I sensed he was becoming out of sorts with himself, with me, and with the whole subject of families. He clenched his fists, and I prepared to duck either a body blow or an uppercut swing of either his right or his left. Instead, he said, "What I don't get," he began in agitation, "is the lack of empathy, or rather compassion, on the part of any of my six and their significant others or their kids, my grandkids, about me. I mean, damn it, if I hadn't made it into my marriage, they'd still be in the queue up there in the sky somewhere waiting for their DNA to be selected so they could enter upon the stage of life."

"But they're not up there in that long line of wannabe babies. They're here, Walter."

"Of course they are, but do they care one iota about me, or are they so self-centered, that the only thing of importance in life is their life."

"It's important to them."

"Of course it is," he readily agreed. "And so to others in their family."

"Like you?"

"And you, Jerry."

I agreed. How could I have disagreed?

Walter was going on, "I mean, I could get run over tomorrow by the Salvation Army collection truck coming for belongings of one of us who didn't make it, and then I wouldn't have made it either, and they'd have to divvy up my possessions, probably six ways, them fighting amongst themselves all the way."

"Walter, their lives are not ours, nor are ours theirs."

"Exactly what I'm saying, but what I want to know is where is their compassion for age, for the frights—the deployment of demons we deal with at two in the morning. You know, the times when you are startled by something within. We wake up, alone, and find ourselves worrying about the morrow, worrying about the state of, or the fall-out or even the definition for our medical conditions—all of them—or else we're worrying about running out of money, our nest egg, sooner or later, maybe sooner, having vanished, and without any realistic means to replenish it—I mean, who's going to hire an 85-year old?" He went on, "And worrying if we're really making the most out of these last years of our lives—however many, or few, there may be remaining for us, or yes, there may be only tomorrow if I get run over by the giant Salvation Army truck or else some old guy in Macrobia who, while driving his Mercedes, suddenly can't remember which pedal is the brake and, with the remaining vigor of his age, hits the accelerator when his car is right in front of me."

I had to echo Walter's concerns, for I, too, had many of the two-AM demons living with me, even though I lived alone. They've ensconced themselves under my bed, there hunkered down in their Maginot Line fortifications. 2 AM is the hour when they come out to feed on aged and seasoned meat. And are they hungry for delicacies! I'm the morsel they spy right off. Ever try to shoo away a hunger demon. They want to dance the demon dance, and if you get out on the dance floor and join them, the sinister, frightening music never stops and pays no heed to the musician's union contracted mandatory break.

Walter wanted to go on and did, "Jerry, think if there's a giant wildfire here in Macrobia, I mean, all of a sudden, and our homes are wiped out and the insurance companies are also wiped out with the magnitude of claims, and they can't or won't pay, and you and I are out on the street, or rather in the adjacent wilderness area with maybe only a sleeping bag if we're lucky, but with no money, no food, no doctors, no car—what do we do? We don't. We die. Piled onto the roving wagons that collect the dead from the disaster; hopefully, I'll be on top of the pile so the TV cameras will catch my image on their news story—my last gasp of notoriety, not that I've ever had any before. He added as a dejected afterthought, "My precious stamp collection never made the news."

"Is that important to you?"

Walter shrugged his shoulders. "Jerry, do our kids, yours and mine, ever care about my worries? No, from my experience with my lot, they don't. My death would mean one less concern for them, that is, if they have any concerns, apart from their own selfish lives."

Walter was depressing me, but I knew he was voicing the deep darks that both of us had, and that I suspected even some of the women in Macrobia were grappling with beneath their cosmetics, hair-dos, and retro fashions. Yes, while we were all walking the streets and paths of Macrobia and talking to others, lurking there for all of us, male and female, were the devilish demons. At least I suspected so. I concluded that each of us, male and female, if the chips were down and the recorder in the confession booth turned on, we each would readily worship the same worries, maybe not daily, but covered up and concealed behind our practiced and rehearsed facades. The concerns were there for us to ponder, the concerns, the laundry lists of dire thoughts occupying our old age lexicon.

Neither of us, I dared say to myself and then out loud to Walter, was prepared to adequately deal with these emotions, even in counseling, for the counselors with whom we might converse were always so young and female. I opined to Walter that we couldn't look to diaries or memoirs of earlier generations for guidance because they didn't live this long. I reminded myself that we were living these long lives thanks to medical advances and stricter dietary regimens, accompanied by the benefits of a tidal wave of knowledge in the new and expanding fields of medical science.

As such, there was no guidebook that I knew of, or that anyone in Macrobia had ever mentioned or cited telling us how to live in our retirement years, in old age—a how-to for elders. None existed; we were each on our own—intrepid explorers suddenly let loose on an uncharted continent, armed only with an employer's pension, social security, or a fat savings account. I blurted at Walter, "Wait, my friend, you're overlooking a vital point here."

He turned his penetrating gaze back at me. I waited. Soon he said, "What me, overlook something?"

I hesitated, he hesitated, and then we each laughed.

"For the first time," I suggested, and more laughter between us.

"Be quick with your admonition," he urged with a smile.

"Seriously," I said, "thing is, we as fathers had something to do with bringing these kids into the world...."

"True, so?"

"So, how long are we responsible for their behavior? Providing financially, yes; providing shelter, yes; providing an education if they want it, yes; providing for their behavior, or determining their behavior once they reach maturity, no!"

"Regrets?"

I shook my head negatively and said, "No, nor do I take any credit for their accomplishments, other than DNA responsibility. I don't put a bumper sticker on my car that says, for example, 'My grandchild is a triple honor student at Studious High School'." I looked back at Walter and said, "They are each their own person, from the day they come into this world. You and I are not their mentors, unless they ask for our guidance, a request I can't remember any of them ever voicing. Their practice is to look to peers and gender heroes for that. So, what they do, their attitudes towards you and me as fathers is their own doing, not ours. In this behavioral category, we get the luck of the draw."

Slowly Walter nodded. To underline, I joined him. Then he said, "The kids, our kids—my six and your three—when you think more about their situations—they don't really have that much of an obligation to their parents or grandparents, now do they?"

"What do you mean?"

"Just what I say. And why should they? It's just family, and families in our culture are disintegrating with remnants floating every which way on the world's air currents, so that you never know where any element is going to be from one year to the next. I mean, they'll say, as one did to me, 'Look, Walter, you fathered us and made enough money so we ate and maybe got into some sort of school, and maybe you helped us with that, and that's that. So, old man, go you own way, whatever that may be. And maybe, like the Eskimos, it's wandering off time into the cold, the real and final cold. So, now I say good-bye to you and yours in your aging years.'"

Thoughtful for a moment about what he'd just said to me, Walter added, "A guy I met here in Macrobia said he co-signed his grandkid's home loan—"

"—A big mistake," I said, interrupting. "Never do that?"

"Student loan?"

"Absolutely not. When your kid defaults, do you want the debt collectors coming after you at your age?"

Walter said, "Even my stamp collection wouldn't satisfy their demands."

"Collectors want cash," I said. "You and I don't want that kind of stress."

CHAPTER 15
OTHERS

Often I replayed in my mind conversations I'd had with other men, and on occasion a few women with whom I had spoken. It was kind of like the replay booth in a football or baseball game, where you could see, and in my case, hear again, at least in my mind, the words that were exchanged.

I'm not sure why I developed this habit, or trait, or maybe a desire. For in my career, I'd just sort of gone along with the flow. I mean, I got instructions from a superior, often the head of the company or the treasurer, or before that time, a boss, and I performed as instructed, to the best of my abilities, and sooner or later was rewarded with a raise in pay, and eventually a pension when I retired. But then Matilda passed away and my focus in life shifted to be seen through a new set of lenses, and it wasn't just the cataract surgery, either. It was a developing desire on my part to understand more about other folks and, of course, myself, in a now single world in which I found myself. That was magnified by my move to Macrobia.

Suddenly other people, their lives, their beliefs, their biases (so I detected) and their worries, and sufferings, became of significance to me. I transformed myself into a sincere listener. Maybe it was the introduction to Buddhism that Walter had led me to. Maybe it was me as I looked back on my life. Maybe it was something else. But it was real. Probably that new interest, new pursuit, allowed me and permitted me to befriend Walter, for I saw in him an opportunity to learn more, much more, about another male human being in carbon copy circumstances, at least location and age wise.

So it seemed to me, as time passed and I had more and more of these experiences, there were few people who reciprocated by appearing to be interested in me. Well, that void didn't bother me, because I was interested in me, naturally, and perhaps that was all that really counted. Walter was curious about me, and for that I was grateful.

Sometimes someone might ask where I was from, and if it was a she, how many children I had. When I said Indiana, their eyes glossed over and they turned to someone else to talk to. Of course, if they were from Indiana—not likely, or so I've become reconciled—we'd have a prolonged conversation about the 500 Mile Race, perhaps, or maybe farming or colleges, or towns, or high schools, or, well, whatever. But that never happened.

I finally concluded, without talking to Walter about the matter, that other people did not share my curiosity, and that was okay, for I could then query them further and learn more about them and their lives and their views and their values, assuming they'd open up to me beyond their cursory replies.

So, I continued to ask, to pry, perhaps, to inquire, to learn more about how to express my curiosity, and hopefully to learn more about the human equation, as it exists in retirement.

The stories were varied. The people were varied. Yet, I'm sure, to younger generations, we all fit into that graying category of mystical pigeonhole of being over the hill in our maturity, our canes and our cares. To them it seemed to be irrelevancies about us unless their financial support was needed. There was no blanket old age picture, not in my mind, but clearly there was in the minds of the younger people, for there lurked a general and mistaken viewpoint, a blurred image, an opaque view, a wrongful realism, a cultural stereotype.

*   *   *

Watching the Game

Six of us—men friends of Walter's and me, that is—were sitting quietly in Walter's living room watching on TV what was known as "The Game." Little was said by any of us, except when a spectacular catch of the quarterback's forward pass was made. Or one time the white-hated referee seemed to appear as if he'd gotten off the bus at the wrong stop, in other words, as confused as we were about the controversial play that had just happened and "the ruling on the field" by the field judge. Immediately, every one of us voiced our own verbal verdict as the replay was replayed time and time again, from all angles, including what appeared to be a camera mounted inside the football as it followed the pigskin's progress as to whether it had indeed touched the ground, or was it real or artificial grass, or pseudo grass, or worse, we didn't care all that much, only waiting for the "ref" to come to his senses and orient himself to the disputed play so that he could decree for all us viewers his all-powerful ruling.

The episode reminded me of thoughts I'd had following Walter's and my conversation about differences between men and women amidst the ancient prehistory hunter-gatherers. Well, of course I didn't know any of those old timers, but I tried to envision their separate gender roles in those early cultures. Here were the brave and hungry guys out chasing some mammoth, or bison, or caribou and trying to bag one or more with their atlatls or spears—probably atlatls because I recall from my one and only class in archaeology that the atlatl was the one invention that probably advanced our species to become what it is today. So, blame the woes of today on the guy—or maybe a gal back then—who invented, or should I say somehow conceived, the concept of the atlatl. I mean, talk about genius! It is a marvelous piece of weaponry, but when I tried to use it, I totally flubbed it, as did everyone else in our classl.

Anyway, trying to imagine life as I envisioned it, lo those many eons ago, I could see and not hear the men in their hunt, communicating with each other only with subdued and quick gestures as to how to position themselves for the kill. Meanwhile back at the encampment, the women were with their children and their chores and, while pursuing those necessities, were constantly talking to each other about, well, about their chores, about their men, and about heaven know what else. Of course, their language was not written, but for sure they understood what each other was saying and gesturing and sounding off on. And I thought about those past evenings in the Events Center with the pervasive female chatter noise as we all waited for the evening speaker to wend through the traffic and begin the talk.

*   *   *

Demographics

The total population of folks living in Macrobia, so the latest issue of our weekly newspaper extolled, was a few short of 15,000. There were, as the paper reported, some 9,000 dwelling units, each owned by one or two senior citizens over the required entry age of 55.

The newspaper's story contained a thesis-like study of the entire population of Macrobia, verbally footnoted and attested to by the Statistic Club's president, who was retired from the United States Census Bureau. She had a number, not a name, and laughed about it when she was introduced by her official numerals. A joke, of course, she assured us, for she was an authorized senior citizen with an authorized name like everyone else residing here.

She gave a class in Macrobia statistics. If the subject was more exciting, I might have been more excited, yet my curiosity about the mix of folks kept me awake as she continued. "Many of the women here are married and living with their husbands; maybe each is a second go-round, either from divorce or death. Many other women are single, widowed or divorced. That leaves the men who are either not married or living with their wives in Macrobia. A lot of other men live alone, either always having been single, divorced, or now widowed."

I thought she had concluded her class, when she looked at me and decreed, "You're single." She added, "On your own."

"Yes," I acknowledged.

"Then you can make friends on your own and not rely on your wife to make the social arrangements."

"Never thought of it that way."

"Yes, our study of the inhabitants here shows that the wives make the social arrangements, always have, and the husband is told where to go and when."

I puzzled. "Why is that?"

"Always been that way in marriage, so our study shows. At least in the generations represented here in Macrobia. Someone else in our club is conducting studies among younger people, and I understand from her the results are quite different."

"How so?"

"Modern marriages are more egalitarian—shared duties, like doing the dishes, scrubbing the floors, and arranging for and hosting the parties."

*   *   *

Walter looked at me hard and smiled. As always, I welcomed Walter's smile, for I knew it was a genuine expression of his friendship. But his smile quickly faded as he demanded that I tell him why we—the two of us—along with so many others at this particular point in our lives were living in Macrobia. "Why is it," he went on, "that we all, each of us, came here to live and cohabitate with so many other older people?"

I felt like saying something about being able to afford it, getting vetted and finally being approved by the all-powerful Board of Directors, forking out the down payment on a villa here, but I said none of that. Instead, I waited, thinking deeply about what might be the intent of Walter's question expressed in that penetrating tone of his, as if I was on the witness stand in a trial and was being required to answer in truth, "so help me God." Yet I remained silent, thinking, searching as to where Walter was going with his insistent question. I was still pondering as to why he was waiting for me to reply and not elaborating on his question or his reason for posing it. Yes, in the silence, the harshness of his abrupt question consumed me, blocking any attempt at conceiving or composing some sort of reply.

Finally, Walter said, "I'm going to ask this question of everyone I come across

throughout the next week."

"Women, too?"

He snorted an "of course" and continued to look at me, waiting for my answer to his for-all query.

Soon I said all the reasons I thought I should have said in the beginning, right after he asked his question: all the many and diverse clubs, the arboretum-like landscaping, the maintenance people on staff taking care of most all home needs....

"No, no, that's not what I mean. Try again."

I did. "I've retired. I have this pension. I worked all my adult life at this large organization. Part of my compensation was this pension of mine. If they hadn't awarded me the pension, I would have taken home a lot more money and probably spent it all by now. As it was, by earning this pension, I didn't spend my retirement prematurely, so now I'm entitled to this pension to pay for my retirement and my health care when medical costs are not covered by Medicare."

"You've got the stock answer, but I say there's more."

"Which is?"

"The truth."

"What then, Walter, do you mean? What do you seek as an addition to my answer?"

"Not yours alone, but everyone's."

"That being?"

"Okay, Jerry, I've been thinking about this question a lot lately, and here is what I've come up with."

I waited, fumbling for my note pad to transcribe Walter's thesis.

In a serious voice, Walter elaborated, "We have each come here to Macrobia because it is meant to be; it is meant for us—you and me and most of the other elders here—that is, for us to be here. And why? Here are the reasons, if you will bear with me."

Walter went on to relate some of the tales he had heard from his male friends in Macrobia. Stories of care, of grief, of bereavement. Stories of strokes. Stories of falls and their insidious repercussions for the person falling, the unexplained fallout from falls, whether down stairs, over curbs, from trying to get out of cars, from ladders, from just losing one's balance and then falling, falling and hitting, hitting, bounding down and down. "Falls can result in broken hips, even concussions," he said, adding, "and even worse."

"Worse?"

Walter nodded reverently. Then he added other stories of care, care for a spouse, care for a child, grown, but still the child with impairment when everything was done medically and compassionately, and nothing worked.

He went on to talk about the years the husband had cared for the wife, through cancer, radiation, memory loss, drugs, pain, pain killers, marijuana biscuits and such. And then came the stroke, after all that. And the loss of voice, but still communicating, still loving. Responsibility to love, to marriage, to a lifetime together. The stories… the stories. And once in a while, things worked, maybe for a short time, but maybe not, yet maybe something new might come along the pike, some new drug, some new technique, some new voice, some new title, some new insight. And the person would be whole again. Just maybe… hope. Just maybe. Yes, hope!

Walter enumerated, "Never before in our history as a species, whether it is Asia, Europe, or the Americas, the Pacific or the Icy regions, have people lived so long as we are experiencing today."

I interrupted. "You're forgetting our Macrobian friends all those centuries ago. You know, the ones the Greek—what's his name— wrote about."

Walter snorted, disdaining my interruption, and then went on, "I am, Jerry, because I'm talking about today. And thanks to exercise, better diet, education, and especially medical science we're all of us, each of us, here in modern day Macrobia, are living longer and longer"

"And doing what with this window in our lives?" I asked.

"Exactly." Walter paused. "But, Jerry, it's not doing, it's exploring. You see, we are all, each of us explorers, like Columbus or whomever you want to hold up as a role model for exploration, whether it be geographic or science, or whatever field. We're all explorers looking into the reasons for and the benefits of human life."

"Meaning?" I Pressed.

"Meaning we need to examine our lives. We've time now—no job, no kids to provide for. We've time, as men in retirement, to delve into ourselves, our own self, explore out own true self, and see what we find. No longer are we compelled to be this or that as defined by our earlier choice of career, choice of job, or categorized by trade, or else by not practicing a trade, but as each of us as an individual human male. This is now our time in which to find out the true self—not the self that appears to others, to society, to the obituary writers, but to ourselves, and to our loved ones. This is why we're here in this retirement place. We've retired from being placed by others into a pigeon hole of where we're from, what we did earlier and during all our life, by how may kids, or wives, or grandkids or cars, or houses, we've got or had, but instead regarded as ourselves, our own selves. And before we can do that, we've got to understand ourselves, we've got to know ourselves."

"Medical science is our savior," I suggested.

"Perhaps," Walter sort of agreed, but went on, "Trouble is today there is so much research going on, resulting in what may turn out to be so many false leads—ideas like a country that prints stamps one day but then is gone and out of being as a country the next—the medical breakthroughs one day may not be the medical breakthroughs on the next day, and their stamps are quickly out of print. And if you're in the field of medicine, the field stretches to the horizon in all directions, and you can't plow or harvest so many fields that stretch—horizon beyond horizon—on and on to scientific infinity."

"The infinity of hope," I suggested.

Walter looked at me, hesitated, and then went on, "So, what may grow in a field, why, we may never find out, yet that particular crop of ideas may be the answer. If not, there is a new field farther on offering more promises of more fertility, bigger and better crops." He paused and slowly added, "Once there, you're lost in the foliage of forever."

I asked, "And how are we going to get beyond these fields of dilemmas in order to accomplish the difficult if not impossible task of knowing what to do, how to deal with our tasks at hand?"

"Right here, Jerry, right here in our own Macrobia. We are the mother lode of this community and it is the place where we are going to delve into these matters. From my experience, that is accomplished through mindful meditation. In the Buddhist fashion. Breathing deeply. In the silence, the silence that comes from being our true selves, it will come to us, and our true self will be revealed to us, by us, and on our own. Through our own efforts, not by taking some pill, not by following some rote memory dogma, not by attending some class—oh, that may help, but in the final sounding of the gong, it is ourselves that must become the explorer."

I chuckled and suggested, "Think of this, Columbus, next time you sail the ocean blue."

Walter added, "Think of this when you walk the paths of Macrobia and sit in the special places reserved for us older people, old men and old women, and all of us not so old in this special place, this retirement community."

CHAPTER 16
MACROBIA'S EVENING'S SPEAKER

From women's eyes this doctrine I derive;
They sparkle still the right Promethian fire;
They are the books, the arts, the academes,
That show, contain, and nourish all the world"
—Shakespeare (Love's Labour's Lost)

The week's Macrobia celebratory festivities continued with a widely-touted evening event held in the overlarge Event Center. For the Healthy Living Club's dinner, the sea of flower-decorated dinner tables were fully occupied with hundreds of seniors—I lost track after counting 400—all of whom were expressing themselves to each other in serious dialogue. As such, rebounding from off the wooden ceiling, the cumulations of the conversations raised the decibel level to the point at which one wondered if there was a max to this escalating chatter that a listener, male or female, could tolerate?

Typical of events in this community, the majority of this evening's attendees were female, mirroring the demographics of the nation's aging population, as well as consistent with Macrobia's gender mix. By now, demographers had researched enough census data to know a lot about older men, for the few they could find to count confirmed their actuarial tabulations that senior men disappear off life's stage at an earlier age than senior women. I'm sitting next to my friend Walter. Our friendship is not based upon respective ages. Except in this place, age mates must be over 55, most over 65, a lot past 70, even 80, and 90-plus. At this stage in my life, I have come to realize that camaraderie of age has become paramount to my daily life. The other six at our table are women. Walter may know them, since he's been here more years than me. Only in a certain few clubs, I have found out, in a total of some 200 organizations, were men in the membership majority—such as the antique car club, the men's golf club, retired professional athletes, and Walter's and my stamp club.

I reflected on the evening's speaker, who was billed as an academic from a think tank affiliated with the nearby state university, obviously an authority on her subject of "Living with Old Age." Her talk had been highlighted on our many kiosks and in our weekly Macrobia newspaper. Were someone to take a survey, from her poster picture, she appeared to be a youngish late 40-something. Her topic was of vital and obvious interest to everyone in the crowded hall, be they female or male.

Club president Jewell Jones pounded her gavel to interrupt everyone's conversation so she could announce the many upcoming club events—date, time, speaker, or discussion topic. She recited which duo of female club members was assigned to bake and bring coffee cake for morning meetings, cookies for those programs scheduled for afternoons, and deserts for the evening events.

Continuing, she then introduced a group of students from the local high school, announcing they would sing, and did, a cappella, "Old Grand Dad," followed by "Grandma's Hands," then "Help the Aged," concluding with "You are My Sunshine, My Only Sunshine." Each title elicited a round of supportive applause from most, and on the last one, given the memories, tears from others.

*　　　　*　　　　*

Caesar Salad

The caterer's personnel began serving the Caesar salads.

Walter tasted, looked at me, and said, "Do you know where the name for this salad came from?"

I didn't know and was pretty sure I didn't care, but well, inasmuch as Walter was about to enlighten me, maybe I did care. Suddenly I did.

"There once was this chef in Tijuana," he began. "His restaurant was popular among the Hollywood types who crossed the Mexican border on their frequent getaway larks. The chef enhanced his greens with a unique dressing he had concocted. His name was Caesar something or other. Enamored with the salad, the Hollywood types pried the recipe from the chef and brought it back to movie land, where the dressing became famous." Walter added, as if to justify his tale, "Everyone knows Hollywood sets trends for the rest of the country and the world."

"How do you know all this, Walter? Or, do you make it up as you go?" I laughed, hoping the waitperson would bring wine as I toyed with an empty goblet.

Walter said he was just reporting for my benefit.

I quipped, "How lucky can a fellow get?"

Walter ignored my caustic remark. He often did that, each time making me feel as if I was a calloused old guy, devoid of sensitivity. I vowed not to do it again, for I valued his friendship and wanted to nourish it.

I almost missed his next story for he was saying, "Jerry, this is related. After the South lost the Civil War, a number of Confederate leaders planned to flee to Mexico. There they would re-form the Confederacy. And," Walter held up his hand as if to signify I was about to benefit from the punch line, "One wealthy plantation owner went so far as to issue a few postage stamps for the new Confederacy. They showed a slave wearing a sombrero while picking cotton."

I laughed and suggested he was making that up, for Tijuana was in Baja, a long way west from Old Dixie. He smiled as his fork dived into his Caesar salad.

By then in our friendship, I'd seen most of his stamp collection, and one of his failed countries was, of course, the actual Confederate States of America. He nodded. "I've lots of these," he had allowed. This evening he stopped eating his Caesar, looked up at me, and as I took my first bite, he said, "I'll tell you something else about the Confederacy you may not know."

Being Walter's friend, I politely urged him on. After all, you investigate a corner of history when you begin to talk or read about topics such as The Old South. The act of peeking in, I have always thought, sparks one's curiosity to know more. So, I anticipated Walter sharing his knowledge, which he promptly did, asking, "Who was the force behind starting the American Civil War?" He expanded, "The War Between the States, or if you choose, The Second War for Independence?"

I raised my eyebrows in query. I often did that when I was at a loss for the right words.

He held up his salad fork and said, "Let me explain about the infamous 45 families of the Old South. They were not like families most of us are familiar with, or a member of. They were the ultra-wealthy ones." He held up his index finger and added, "Today we'd label them as the top one tenth of one percent of the population." He went on to explain that they owned the plantations and almost all of the slaves. "In the fallout of the 1860 presidential election, these families had the most to lose from the Republican presidency of Abraham Lincoln. These wealthy families were the exclusive planter class that effectively ran the Lower Southern states during the break-away secessionist sentiment in the years leading up to the Civil War."

I listened as Walter continued, "As a result of Lincoln being elected, they feared losing everything—their slaves, land, plantation homes, valuable possessions. They would go bankrupt. You see, they owed a lot of money to banks in the North and in England. Under Lincoln's feared freeing of their slaves, this planter class of 45 families would never be able to pay back their creditors. Their slaves were their means to generate income from their vast plantation holdings. Without slave labor, they'd have no one to do the hard work of farming to grow the cotton, tobacco, or sugar. In the aftermath of Lincoln's election, they believed they would lose big time." Perhaps lamenting a sea change in the culture of the Old South, Walter went on to predict that the plantation owners' way of life would be gone with the wind. He said, "Accordingly, they all agreed that they had no choice but to fight for Southern independence from the Union in order to retain their system of government, preserve their wealth, and continue their coveted lifestyle as the 45 dominant ruling families of the Old South." As he finished off his Caesar salad, Walter appended, "The normal people of the Old South, the regular folks, the yeoman farmers, the white workers—did not have a chance to vote to secede from the Union. It was the people in power—these 45 families with their lands, their slaves, their influence over each state legislature, including bribes—they're the 45 families who started the American Civil War."

I had stopped eating to listen to Walter. I wondered why Walter had learned all this from his postage stamp collection. What mental force had driven him to learn so much? I wanted to expand my understanding of the world, too. Isn't that every young boy's dream, his motivational desire in life? Mine certainly had been, as I reflected back on my childhood. As adults, we don't lose that desire, or do we?

But this dialogue with Walter tugged at me, urging me, requiring me to know more about him. He was a friend. Aren't we always more curious about our friends? Or are we? Do we just accept them and go on? Or do we wonder if we are like them and they like us, and is that the mutual attraction of our intellects? For having joked together, commiserating when appropriate, didn't I want to know more about Walter? Yes, I knew I did.

*   *   *

Once more Jewell Jones, was tapping the microphone to get everyone's attention. Not easy in the din of dinner talk. With partial success in her mission, she re-introduced herself and said she must apologize for a brief delay in serving the "main course of our dinner," as the chef had not yet arrived in the hightech kitchen adjacent to the large dining room. He was delayed in traffic, she advised, "But in his tweet, he assured me he'd be here within the quarter hour." In the interest of acknowledging culinary values, she explained, "The chef's approval of each plate before delivery to our loyal club patrons is essential. It is our rule for hosting a dinner party." Silver and baldheads nodded in unison, expressing their agreement. As Jewell Jones returned the microphone to its holder, the room buzz resumed.

CHAPTER 17
THE COUNTRIES

Old Age is the most unexpected
of all things that happen to a man
—Leon Trotsky

Still no diner was being served, but the Caesar salad had fortified me enough to continue my conversation with Walter, and he with me, at least during the intermission wait.

Walter was saying, "Jerry, the other evening you asked me a question, but I don't think I answered it correctly or fully."

"Do you ever?"

"Do you?"

"Always. Of course. Doesn't everyone?"

"That's my point."

"Which is?"

"These countries, whose stamps I collect, never made it—well, there's no spokesperson left for them to answer the basic question as to why they didn't make it into the League of Nations, or later the UN, NATO, the European Union, or LATS—"

"—What's that?"

"The League of Awful Terrorist States…"

I interjected, "Or whatever is the organization du jour for countries."

Walter smiled and nodded. "You could say it that way, I suppose."

I suggested, "There's no one to speak for them? Is that what you are saying?"

"True, other than historians… or… well, me."

"They all thank you, Walter." I laughed.

He scowled. "And that's my point, if you'll allow me to make it."

I motioned for him to go ahead on it, and he did. Walter elaborated, as follows. I think I can recall most of what he said, although it is rather long in detail and a bit abstract. But then I'm pretty good, I tell folks, on abstract concepts. I like abstractions better than actual factual statements, which can be chunked away at like a bird on an apple, or a tree, such as a determined woodpecker. But abstractions are like clouds in the sky: you can't abstractly peel off a piece and chew on it, not like you can with fixed absolutes.

*   *   *

Walter was starting to explain his point to me when his dinner plate was placed on the table before him. He looked annoyed at the waitperson for the fragrance of the broccoli florets had sidetracked his conversation. Nevertheless, he eyed the beef and bit into the first slice, smiled at the French chef-seasoned taste, and said, "Just think, Jerry—"

"—I always do," I said.

Ignoring me, as a good friend can do without offending, Walter went on: "My point, Jerry, is that there are quite a number of these long-gone states, such as the Confederacy and Epirus—well, I can go on and on—"

"—Yes, I know, and I want you to." Walter seemed pleased with my emotional support, voiced with a round of butternut squash ravioli in my mouth.

He continued, "For now, as my example, I'll stick to Epirus."

Though I knew, I prodded Walter—mean of me, I suppose, but then friends can be joyfully mean with friends, or so I thought at this moment. Maybe I was wrong, and, if so, I moved toward a mindset of regret, but anyway I said, "Walter, my friend, I do know where Epirus is, or was, but tell me, what do you think Epirus represents? I mean, what does its story tell us today about countries, perhaps about ourselves... well, about anything?"

"Everyone knows—"

"—No one knows," I corrected. I'll bet you a bite of beef that I can go table to table in this Event Center and no one, and I mean no one will know about Epirus, or why I'm even asking."

"Well, then I'll tell you."

"You're on, Dude."

"Guy is better. I like 'Guy' better."

"Okay, Guy, go"

Walter took out his pen and, on the paper tablemat—a peg down from the dish offering the chef's culinary presentation—he began to draw a map, shoving his tablemat, dinner plate on top, toward me so I could better see his artwork.

"Greece!" I exclaimed recognizing the outline of the Peloponnesus and lands to the north.

Walter continued his pen action, pointing. "And here is Albania."

"Yes, for my stamp collection, I know about King Zog." I added, "Once part of the Ottoman Empire."

He nodded. "All this Balkan land was part of it for long centuries." He thought and appended, "Muslim."

We ate in silence for a few moments while I reviewed this bit of geography and history, wondering all the while why Walter was so engrossed in this particular story, not only this one, but apparently a bevy of other similar stories about countries or wannabe countries. I dared ask as much.

Walter quipped, "I thought I had explained it to you, Jerry?" His tone was simply a matter of fact, not in criticism, although among friends one might construe it as a take down, an attempt at a jab that might humble the recipient into a state of self-criticism for being so out of it. But being his friend, I knew that was not his intention. It was that I didn't understand his motive, which, of course, I didn't. So, in my friendly way, I said to Walter, that is, after another bite of the ravioli, which was, after all, quite good, helping me to understand this complex man, my friend. I implored, "After you've devoured your beef and broccoli florets, I am hoping you will explain yourself further. As your friend, I want to know."

Walter nodded.

The waitperson served a round of pinot noir for our table, women included; some declined and wanted white—chardonnay, they each, in succession, ordered. Except for one woman who I could see holding her bejeweled hand over the empty glass signifying her non-participation in the pour. Walter and I toasted our red wine glasses in our own private exchange, saluting the expression we voiced simultaneously, "To our good intentions!"

"You see," he began, there were people in Epirus who wanted an independent little enclave to add to the partitions—the breakups—of what was becoming of the once mighty Ottoman Empire." He added, "These were real people. With real desire, and real ambitions. Real Plans. Albeit persons who, alas, were economically ill-advised, at least by measuring with our standards of both academic and practical economics today, but that was back before there was much of a study of what made a country tick—the region's economic base—you know, statistics of commerce. "

"Took a course in statistics once," I offered.

"Dull as dirt," he opined, "but an understanding, even if rudimentary, is necessary if one is to follow events today." He moved his empty dinner plate away from the artwork on his tablemat and pointed his pen at the area he had marked as Epirus—on the border of present-day Albania and Greece. "You see, Jerry, there were people here, people like you and me—oh, they spoke one of the two Albanian dialects, maybe Greek, maybe folk dialects; that's not the point, but they didn't get their nation. And so, they had to go back to being farmers, tailors, schoolteachers, maybe some other means of livelihood, and live their lives either in Albania or in Greece. That is, until World War II, when…"

I interrupted to tell Walter that in my stamp collection I had a number of Albanian stamps. I went on to describe the famous issue, a set of King Zog and Queen Geraldine at their coronation in 1938. "That was," I said, "nine months before Mussolini invaded Albania on Good Friday and took over the country. "Geraldine was American," I told Walter. "She delivered their baby as Italy's fascist dictator, Il Duce, was landing his troops."

"Real people," Walter commented.

"From North Carolina," I mentioned.

"Who?"

"Geraldine."

Sometimes among friends, it is not necessary to acknowledge every comment, every statement. Being friends, it is assumed the friend gets it and, because you are friends, it is not necessary to go overboard polite. In this case, Walter said nothing, so as the plates were being cleared, I went on with my questioning, "Walter, what attracted you to places like Epirus, and how many more did you say there are like Epirus, countries that no longer exist but that have stamps you collect?"

He had retrieved his tablemat and folded it neatly into what I presumed he would regard later as a pocketsize memo of our conversation. As he was inserting it into his inside blue blazer pocket, he looked over at me, pointed at his blazer and said, "Nordstrom's had a sale. I'm a sucker for sales there."

"I'm a Wal-Mart shopper," I said sheepishly and waited for him to reply to my question.

"Nordstrom's reminds me of some of the people in some of these out-of-business countries whose stamps I collect."

"That's a stretch," I said in judgment. "After all, you can't go back, way back into history, with your analogies, because stamps didn't begin until—what was it?—1840, or thereabouts for the first honest-to-goodness postage stamp. Of course, there was postal service earlier."

"Yes," he agreed, adding, "via stage coach and ships' captains."

"Pony Express, too," I suggested. "Still do it, I'm told, once every year in Arizona—a real re-enactment. Never seen it though."

"I have," Walter boasted. "I may be old in this retirement neighborhood of ours, but I'm not that old to have witnessed the original pony express back in, what was it?"

"A long time ago," I suggested.

Walter laughed heartily and I with him. He added, "If I were that age, I'd be, by far, the oldest old guy in Macrobia."

"You're sure of that? You know, there's a club here restricted to those who are 100 or older."

"Yeah, I know." Walter laughed and then was quiet for a moment, his laugh wearing off into what I surmised to be sort of a state of oblivion.

I reflected on the status of a discarded laugh as I puzzled over his statement, a statement wrought with side effects, both emotional and chronological. Talk of age, old age, getting older, and living with age on a daily basis had become at this point in my life to be a subject I shunned, a topic I'd rather not bring up, or respond to if someone else did mention it, which was often daily, and often multiple times each day, not by me but by others obsessed with its meaning, its varied effects on them, on each of us.

So, I poured myself a half-glass of the red wine from the bottle left on our table by the attentive waitperson. I sipped and then put down the glass. "Cool it," I said to myself, and wished Walter had not brought up the age thing. But drinking more wine wouldn't make it go away. Nothing would. And I knew that. And Walter knew that. And everyone in this giant room, male and female, knew that.

Walter and I had talked about age, our respective ages. More than once, that's for sure, as most of us find we have to do to be in a Macrobian conversation, so it seemed to me, sitting at our dinner table in that huge room with so many other aged folks, I knew one could initiate a conversation with almost anyone, even females, by mentioning what I had come to dread in conversations as "the chorus of aging factor."

CHAPTER 18
THE SPEAKER TELLS ABOUT AGING

Growing anxious about the evening's event, Walter raised an of the moment question, "When is our guest speaker going to speak?" He answered himself, "Soon, surely," He laughed, as Walter can laugh. His is a deep knowing laugh, like he knows more about the humor than he's sharing, and if you give him a chance, he'll disclose that insight.

I gave him the chance by remaining silent and looking at him directly.

He said, "You know, Jerry, I don't think I want to know any more about aging. In fact, truth be told, I want to know less. If I could become a Know-Nothing, like that political party in the 1860 presidential election, maybe I'd be better off. Maybe, if they'd won the presidency instead of Lincoln, the Confederacy would never have been born. Just think of all the lives that would have been saved, well, not saved but not lost. It would have been up to each one of the people alive then, individually, to save themselves, as it is with each of us, don't you think?"

Walter delivered his rant with gusto and, in response, one wonders if one should not respond, but instead grunt or nod or clap or else do nothing, allowing the pontification to sink in, given your respect for the pontificator. After all, he or she, as the case may be, had to have thoughts about his or her statement before delivering it. Don't you think so? I mean, I do and did, so I was silent. But only for a moment. I had to ask, "Walter, tell me, dear friend, on another but vital subject, did you always yearn to make money, I mean, a lot of money in your career, in your life? Well, I guess you didn't have a career, but rather a series of events, a pathway in life that was quite different, I mean not less important, perhaps more important, for in my opinion you contributed yourself to society; I simply went along for the ride, and I might say, rode the wagon well."

"But aging? You know, Jerry, I never thought much about aging. It just came upon me, the advancing years, coming at me year after year. But you, you've thought about it, analyzed it, asked questions about it, read about it, talked about it, and you are the one that dragged me to this event this evening." Walter's laugh came at me once again, this time like a dart throw.

I was upset at Walter's barb. I hadn't "dragged" him here. Or had I? I mean, one doesn't drag a friend around. But would I have come by myself, given the hordes of women attending here tonight, not knowing many of them, sitting by myself with a table of seven of them, none talking to me, and I not to any of them? Probably not, but I did want to hear what the speaker had to say about aging, and I felt sure so would Walter have wanted to hear, and I was disappointed in what he said, and in his tone of voice he used to express his thoughts to me.

Wanting to change the subject, I again asked him about his youthful, and maybe even adult craving for making money.

"Oh, yes," he replied, as if he was on automatic response, "aren't we all driven by the lure of riches of the American Culture? The drive to make money is pervasive in our male lives. We each want to become another Horatio Alger, that newspaper boy who became a millionaire."

"Billionaire, today," I corrected, then went on, "But, Walter, I wasn't so obsessed with making money." I thought and then asked myself out loud, "Or was I?" It was then that I asked Walter, "Do you think, therein lies the major difference between you and me?" I added as an afterthought, "Are you and I any different from the few men here tonight? And the vast number of women? Did any of them, growing up as a little girl, want to make money in their lives? Did they fantasize about becoming rich on their own, with their own ideas, their own wits, their own monetary drive, yielding to the consuming lifetime incentive of the lure of riches? I mean, apart from simply marrying a wealthy male?"

Walter's reply bordered on decreeing to me, "such a stupid question" as he said, "How would I know?"

"Or I?"

"Neither of us will know any of those answers," Walter concluded.

I pondered his opinion with growing skepticism.

Walter must have read my thoughts, for he said, "Jerry, let's do our own survey right here and now."

"At our table?"

Walter didn't answer. Instead, he stood, tapped his water glass with the edge of his spoon. It took a moment for table silence to muffle the decibel level. Waiting, and when it was time, Walter spoke in a soft and Walter-friendly voice to our opposite-gender tablemates: "Ladies, Jerry here and I would like to ask each of you a question."

In response, the six women looked at Walter, then at me, and then back at Walter, as if they were carrying out a female drill maneuver. One seemed to me to be annoyed at their female conversation banter had been trumped by a male. The others, so I thought, were curious at the meaning of the interruption. They waited. One finished her wine and promptly smiled up at Walter, as if she welcomed this male intrusion to their female world.

Walter smiled and instructed, "Going from left to right," and he gestured at the woman sitting to my left, "I'd like to ask you, as I go around the table, one simple question that will help Jerry and me to better understand our lovely Macrobia women."

Several smiled up at Walter, suggesting their comfort with the episode. However, one said, "You can drop the 'lovely.' We're all, each of us, a Macrobia woman, plain and simple."

Walter nodded and smiled in agreement. He went on to explain further, "Jerry and I are discussing and disagreeing with each other perhaps, as to whether, as kids, we yearned to make a lot of money in our lives. Jerry suggested women never entertain such ambitions. I disagreed. So, I'd like to ask you, starting with—" and he gestured to the woman to my left.

"Lilly" was the name she told us.

Walter nodded and queried, "Lilly, did you as a young girl or woman entertain fantasies or desires or plans about making a lot of money in your life, in a career? That's what I want to ask each of you in turn."

Lilly shook her head and replied, "No, I never entertained such thoughts. Instead I saw myself becoming a teacher, maybe an actress, neither of which in my day were paths to riches by any means, at least not like they may be now. Yet, I felt those ambitions were laudable, even if somewhere along the line I did get married and have children."

*   *   *

I couldn't help it, but at that moment my mind began to wander uncontrollably across my emotional archives. I was going back almost 70 years to 1950 and the start of the Korean War with its compulsory military draft. Suddenly I was faced with the threat, indeed the probability, of being forced into the American Army, taught to kill, and then quickly sent off to war halfway around the globe, to fight for what was at that time a rather corrupt South Korean government of a so-called ally, which was a so-called democracy. To go there against my will, contrary to my developing plans for my life ahead, trained and told to fight against communism as represented by that the half-country's invading army from the North that was expressing unfettered military aggression with its tanks, jet planes, and soldiers, who were marching across an arbitrary geographic line on a faraway peninsula. Not in a declared war, but in what became officially known in our country as a "Police Action."

Meanwhile women, like those at our diner table, were free to embark on their marriages or their careers, if they so perceived such a life promise. They weren't being drafted. They weren't being forced against their will into boot training. They weren't learning how to fire a rifle, drive a tank, fly a jet fighter plane, all the while being taught to kill other human beings, other men, and maybe in the process women and children on the ground who happened to have gotten in the way of the righteous fight against communism.

Men were being schooled in how to battle like it must have been in the crusades, all for a better, a higher, a God-supported cause to rid the world of infidels, of those who would destroy "us." Of those who would destroy our Capitalist system, even though by at that age I had not reaped any benefits from this Capitalist system, while owners of the factories making the armaments, all the supplies, were banking their dividends and enjoying the riches of Capitalism. Why had I awakened to servitude, locked into to a system I was trying to understand, meanwhile reading about other belief systems offered in other parts of the world? Spiritualism was being pursued everywhere except in the United States. I felt fear and trepidation, let alone disappointment.

Was it the abuses of a religion practiced by the Capitalist system, whilst elsewhere in the world—for example, among Native Americans in our own country other and much different philosophies flourished, both in spirituality and with different sets of beliefs, all of which we were being trained to shun, to ignore, and even to ridicule. But, without the opportunity to explore these beliefs, these different systems, how could we be forced into an army of soldiers that was being ordered to kill they who are not us, they who believe something "other?"

*   *   *

The woman past Lily, whom I had heard over my aberrant mind's ruminations, said her name was Rose. She told us, "When I was in high school, I had an interest in chemistry. If I were to go on to college, I told myself I would major in chemistry, not because I might make a lot of money—not at all—I was interested in working in the field, discovering things, and maybe, just maybe making a contribution to science. But my guidance counselor kept telling me to just simply stick with school 'til you get married, and then your husband will be the breadwinner, and you can have your kids.' That was the message repeated time and again by teachers, by my friends who were doing just that, or wanting to, and so, when the whole world tells you something, you begin to believe you are wrong, mixed up, improperly motivated, and the world is right."

Walter asked, in his usual polite tone of voice, "And you did just that?"

Rose replied, "Yes." She covered her face. And I knew, as did all of us at the table, Rose was stifling tears.

My mind moved off of myself as I thought of my sister, who was born before I was. She had told me more than once she wanted to be an aviator, emulate Amelia Earhart. She had tried to take flying lessons, but the male instructors just wanted to take her up and take her down—that's all. I loved my sister. She finally got married, had a little boy and gave him nothing but toy airplanes to play with. She's passed on now.

*   *   *

Walter thanked Rose and smiled at the next woman, urging her to go ahead. Her name was Sharon. Meanwhile, my thoughts went back to the Korean War and the compulsory military draft. I remembered considering ways to dodge the draft.

One was to try to enroll in divinity school. I had always been interested in the subject, as I was with a lot of subjects, especially postage stamps. I was interested enough in organized religion to be able to fill out the application and probably get a recommendation from the pastor at my parent's place of worship.

The local draft board authorities were granting deferments for religious schools. So, I could get a PhD divinity degree and pretend I wanted to save souls. But I didn't know what a soul was. And besides, if I were going to minster to veterans returning from the war—or to the families of those lost in the war—excuse me, Police Action—how could I possibly empathize with any of them, for I would never have experienced the military, the battlegrounds, the weapons, the fear, the death of comrades. Let alone the enemy. How could I hold myself out as a spiritual leader, given those handicaps of creditability? The religious robes, the religious paraphernalia, the hymnals, the sermons about Bible stories—would any of those props

104

make up for a zero as to my feelings, for a naught on my empathy, for a nada on my ability to commiserate with those who had been there in the war or those relatives who had lost loved ones. The answer was a zip. Simply to recite church doctrine, without having experienced empathy, was not going to do it for me.

I had also thought about going to Canada, as were a number of my friends; at least we were talking about such a move. Of course, as I had earlier confided to Walter, that was what I did do. In the intellectual exploration of this idea, my thoughts ran along these lines: What good could I possibly do for society if I were killed in Korea? Oh, sure, I'd have a military funeral to the tune of taps, played ever-so reverently. I would have "done my duty," "served my country," "be forever entombed with other patriots in some Veterans Administration cemetery," my forever site looked after, perhaps occasionally a flower or two placed thereon. I respected those already there; no quarrel with them, but of course they weren't able to quarrel any more with me or with anyone, their deed of death having been done.

My dreams, and I had had dreams in those days, were of a career in which I would make money and, in the process, contribute my part toward a peaceful society. Those were thoughts every boy in those days entertained from having read Horatio Alger, or at least knowing the story, which in those days was part of the American male sinew. Clearly, in hindsight and at the time, as well, the draft and the war stymied my career, forced it to be shelved, while I dealt with the draft.

What was the effect, if any, for females? With no draft to face, they could go on with their lives and their hopes. Walter was trying to find out answers, while I was selfishly thinking my own thoughts, which focused ever so briefly on a child I'd had out of wedlock, a baby girl. But I set her aside once again and focused back on our table conversation.

I wanted to hear from the other women at our table, to listen to Walter's queries and their contributions to our little discussion, which by now expanded to an 8-persons-at-the-table. Having recalled what had happened to me, I wondered about Walter. Was in the military?

A year older than me, he had to have been subject to the draft, just as I had been.

*   *   *

The third woman, Mary Lou, told us that she was not interested in making a lot of money. That's what fathers are for," she said. "At least that was my feeling back then. Keep in mind, we're talking 50 to 60 years ago, not today. Today is different. My granddaughter wants to make tons of money. She's got her degree in computer science and is working for a tech startup in Silicon Valley. What else do we expect our daughters to do today? Certainly not get married and have a family. At least not yet in their lives, once they're into college and then, whisk, out of school and determined to find a job in order to make a lot of money."

The other women applauded Mary Lou, echoing her sentiment. But then the next woman, whose name was Marsha, said she faced her life with determination to marry a successful man as soon as one came along. She laughed, and added, "Even with jobs in nursing and hospital administration, I'm still waiting." She laughed and asked, "Are either of you two men successful and rich?" The other women laughed, as did Walter and I. "Not me," I said. Walter nodded, holding out both arms simulating an embrace of her.

Fleetingly I took in Marsha's appearance, her smile, what I perceived to be her warmth toward Walter, even if in jest. She was, well, I didn't know her age, but like all of us here, she was in the third half of her life. And, for a moment, I speculated what it might be like to, somehow—and I wouldn't know how to do it—develop a relationship with a female here in Macrobia, you know, a significant emotional relationship.

Would it, could it ever work? Would I want it? Would I ever pursue it? How could it work? Each of us probably recalled from our earlier lives, somewhere in our minds, not entirely lost in our memories, our thoughts, our emotions, coming together, sharing in depth with each of us, as I had shared in my marriage with Matilda all those years, those years of raising three kids, or trying to. My mind, then and now, was full of doubts, of reservations, haunted by a fear of failure, with the hope of success only an opaque and distant light from a faraway dim light bulb. What would be success? What would work? Puzzling, I waited in silence for Walter to continue his exploration of female motives toward making money.

The sixth woman, Sharon, was beginning to voice her opinion, "My family was well off in those days. My father was a successful merchant in our town, and so I was sent to business school to learn merchandising. That became my career—turning merchandise into money. I did well at it, if I may say so. So, yes, I guess you might say I was oriented to making money. In retrospect, I will tell you my motivation went beyond money. It was to devote my life to be of service to my family, my father and mother, and then later, when I married, to my husband, who didn't understand much about the business, and later to our two children who did. It was family first for me."

Walter and I thanked our tablemates, as each of us at the table toasted each other, a welcome gender bonding salute in this female tilted community.

CHAPTER 19
WHERE ARE YOUR CHILDREN TODAY?

*...children at play are not playing about; their games should be seen
as their most serious-minded activity.*
—*Lady Mary Worley Montagu, 1689-1762*

Jewell Jones was announcing that the speaker had just tweeted she was delayed in traffic but expected to arrive "momentarily." I thought she might better add, "hopefully." Jewell apologized for the delay, and then went on to describe the news she had picked up on her tablet about a 10-car pileup on Interstate 680, with all lanes closed by the highway patrol, ambulances and wreckers on their way to the scene. The delay, which I presumed would go on longer than Jewell had predicted, gave me time to think back about one evening Walter and I enjoyed at our old stagecoach stop.

He had ordered us each a beer and then spoken to me in his subdued voice—quietly so that no one else in the bar would hear, and there were a number of oldies drinking there that evening, in fact quite a few. I could see that he knew several, for he waved at one and nodded at others before he leaned closer and began his story.

"Six kids, he said. "Four are mine—two boys and four girls. The boys are not mine."

"Whose, then?" I asked as gently as I could, then suggesting, "Adopted?" That was what I thought to be the alternative to births from a marriage.

"My wife's," he allowed.

I puzzled. "Before your marriage?"

"Don't I wish?" He ground his teeth, but soon continued, "We had a rocky go of it at times, sometimes for extended periods. Our marriage was like some of my collecting countries—vibrant one day, but then turning to duplicates for, as we say in stamp lingo, "traders" with other collectors at shows and meetings."

I waited, uncomfortable about saying anything further to my friend; besides, I didn't quite know what to say, yet I felt I needed to say something, but like a lot of situations in life, there is seldom a handy guidebook to which to refer for instructions. Yet, of course, I was curious to learn more, but then I asked myself why was I curious? After all, it's Walter's life, his privacy, his doings, and his emotions at stake. Who am I to pry, to ask, to intrude, to want to know?

I supposed, as I sat there in silence, one wants to know about others so that one may learn, adding to their own selfish education about life. After all, if so and so dealt with such a problem and he or she shares with me their mindset at the time, I might learn how to deal in the future with comparable situations in my life that could arise. My life might then be happier. Or not. Or maybe in empathy, I'd be down and unhappy, or feel compassion for the other person's tribulations, and I'd be sharing in their suffering. Yet, I had learned that compassion is not sharing, not sitting in their socks, but instead, respecting their suffering, and letting them know of your concern for their eventual or immediate enlightenment. At least you could demonstrate to them that you were listening and caring, as a friend ought to do.

My thoughts were trumped by Walter whispering words about his kids, "I try, Jerry, to maintain a semblance of communication with each of them. But it's one out of six—that's my batting average. The one who comes up to the plate regularly tries to get the others and their spouses, when they have a spouse, into the program with names and numbers and email addresses and align them in some sort of batting order. But, alas, the program never gets printed or even a draft handed out at the occasional so-called "family" get-together, "corrections invited just to keep us all up-to-date." I submitted, "Today in this country families no longer stay together in their home town—what we once referred to as 'our town'—not in today's world."

"Worse," Walter worried, "being so distant from one another, they are not likely to feel responsibility to each other."

"Or to the family as an entity," I blurted to Walter's reluctant nod and his ensuing words of lament, "On three Continents…."

I waited, contemplatively, then queried, "Do you want to tell me about your family?"

"The six?"

I nodded, then asked, "First, will you tell me about your wife, the mother?"

Walter held up his hand, advising, "First, to do this right, we need to start with some ancestors."

"Why," I asked.

"Who we are," Walter advised, "begins with where we've come from, ethnically, geographically, and personality-wise. We are a product of all that, plus our own uniqueness. That's my opinion, Jerry, so take it for what it's worth."

"Coming from you, it's got worth," I opined.

"Thank you," he said humbly.

"The wife?"

"Married 45 years. She's passed away."

"I'm sorry," I suggested softly.

Walter nodded. "I am, too… usually."

I raised my eyebrows.

"She had two affairs, as you've surmised."

I waited, not knowing what to say. I mean, what does one say? Then I asked, "Which of your kids are you closet to?"

Without hesitation, Walter said, "William."

"He's where?"

"Boston."

"And does?"

"Professor, tenured, Boston College. History. Sixteenth Century or thereabouts, he tells me."

"Fascinating."

"Not really."

"To him."

"I'm sure it must be. He tells me tidbits about the Medici family."

"Are you close… beyond history's little tidbits?"

"Not really."

"A parallel to…?"

Walter thought for a moment. "Like my countries in my collection—families, I mean. Some survive. Some don't make it. Some go extinct and stop printing stamps, or had never even begun to design them. They stop sending messages, stop caring, stop interacting with other families, stop doing business with other families. It all fits a pattern, don't you see?"

I asked, "A pattern of longevity? Of fitness? Of leadership? Of determination?" Then I suggested, "Perhaps all of the above." Or so I expressed to him, while not really understanding, not knowing. I don't like to say things that I don't really know, but then it's like running a flag with a strange device up a flagpole and waiting to see if anyone writes a national anthem for it, salutes, and, well… I don't know what else. Maybe in reaction, young men want to don a uniform, grab a gun and go to war for the banner. I supposed that's how you find out if they print postage stamps. I waited, hoping Walter might clarify my aimless mental wanderings.

"Families are like countries," Walter told me. "Some make stamps—very few, I say. They're the families you collect, the families to which you want to belong. They have love, camaraderie, mutual respect. Otherwise they don't endure. Nor do they even have the wherewithal to paste their own stamps onto the life of the locality."

I asked, "If you could, how would you design the perfect family?"

Walter chuckled, which he didn't often do. With him, it was either a frown or an outright guffaw. But now I was privy to one of his rare chuckles. "It was done in olden times," he declared. "In olden towns and villages. Back when towns were a defined area and the countryside began at the edge of town. In medieval times, that was out beyond the city walls and known as the 'suburbs.' There, farms were proper farms and everyone farmed in the family farm. If you want to go on a treasure hunt today, Jerry, find me a family farm and a farm family living there and cohesively working the farm. And I'll award you the grand prize of last day of issue."

I waited and then queried Walter, "Your kids—nowadays?"

"Like I said, three continents, six countries. Today a family get-together is an email or text, sometimes answered, sometimes not. And when answered it is with, maybe, politeness, or more likely indifference. It's like a marathon of trains. Everyone running along its own track. The engineers and conductors not even waving to one another as they race past each other."

CHAPTER 20
A LIFE

Old Men are Testy,
And will have their way
—Percy Bysshe Shelley (a very young person at the time)

Back at our table for the evening talk in the Event Center, Walter looked at me hard. He shook his head in a strong negative message. "Jerry, you miss my motive."

"Stamps, now, you're speaking of stamps?" I queried to his nod as he went on, "My life has been like these countries that no longer qualified for the authorized postmark of nationhood. I lost the game of growing up, and now play the game of posing as a retired man on campus. So, we have a lot in common. I mean, these countries and me. That's why I collect their stamps. Reminds me of myself. My life. My ambitions. And then, well, I guess I'd have to acknowledge my eventually losing out."

"But you didn't lose out, Walter. Not from the things you've told me."

Walter smiled as if I had hit the nail on the head and said, "I'm like Newfoundland."

"How so?" I felt I was getting to the heart of matters with Walter. I had found Walter to have a big heart. That means for our friendship that he's likable, warm...

"...Well, both the country of Newfoundland and me were going along pretty well. They had issued a lot of stamps as an independent nation, while at the same time I felt I was becoming independent by artfully playing the Capitalist game of 'Greed and money first.' But after World War II, their economy went into the dumps."

As Walter elaborated, I began to remember those days. Going on, Walter said, "As for me, events in tandem, I was out of a job and living off my savings. So, Newfoundland and I—each of us voted to change. In an election, they voted themselves into Canada, and I voted myself back into the community college to see if I could learn how to re-orient my life's goals.

"What had gone wrong?"

"With me or with Newfoundland?"

"You, silly. You're my friend. I don't know jack about Newfoundland."

Walter said something about Leif Erickson and the Vikings discovering the remote island years ago and establishing what he assumed to be a colony there.

"Viking explorers," I managed, trying to verbalize support of Walter.

He pined for a moment, pensive, seemingly pondering his life. He waited until the apple pie alamode was served, smiled at the presentation and said, "I soon gave up on the community college program and began speculating in real estate. It was my scheme to get rich, and to do so quickly and with ease, or so I made myself believe. I signed up for a course from this hotshot known as the 'Flipper Whale—you can make a whale of a lot of money by splashing your fins like me'. That was the pitch for the courses he offered and the how-to books he sold to people like me who fancied making big money quickly and easily. He displayed photographs of happy graduates from his course. They were fashionably attired and smiling next to their expensive sport cars or else lounging on the beach at some exclusive Caribbean resort."

"Did it work?" I asked, having only a cursory idea what he was talking about. You see, I'd had this career, from which I had retired after 35 years of taking the only risk I had to, and that was driving to work every day. "Boring," I said to myself about myself, not exciting like each of Walter's new ventures. For the moment I was envious of him.

"Your life or mine?" Walter's tone of voice was edged.

"Your life, of course," I assured him.

Vilified, Water went on, "The scheme sort of worked the first time. I got a lot of itemized income tax deductions from paying his course fees, interest on the money I borrowed from the mortgage lender, property taxes paid to the county, and the money I spent to rehab an old apartment house. But then, well, by now you may see the fallacy in the scheme. I didn't have a lot of income from which to deduct the deductions. But the second time…."

"Wait. You sold your first venture, what should I call it?"

"Flipper Number One." Walter replied, hesitated, and added, "Yeah, I sold it. Broke even, well, sort of."

I interrupted his investment tale to flip my own stroke, but then wished I hadn't quipped what I shot at him, "Sort of' must mean 'no.'"

He replied sheepishly, "Yeah."

"Sorry, I was being flippant."

Walter was silent, using the time to devote his attention, perhaps in welcome divergence, to his mouthful of pie and ice cream. Two bites. As did I, wondering what went wrong with the flipper whale's splash into the quick money game.

Soon Walter answered my silent question. "You see, the state where I was living imposed no sales taxes, so communities got their revenue to run their governments and their schools from property taxes assessed on real estate, such as my apartment building. Of course, when the county assessor noticed my improvements, in his or her mind the value of the building went up with the last carpet installation, and with it, my property tax assessment escalated. The beloved tax assessor, making notes into his tablet computer, days later doubled my property taxes."

I suggested, "Flipper the Whale's promise had many dimensions."

Walter nodded. "But wait, Jerry, there's more bad news. Without warning or an alarm bell sounding, rents all over town started to soften."

"How can rents soften?" I asked, revealing my lack of knowledge of real estate investment. I'd always owned my house, never rented. Didn't know what that was like.

Rents can go down because of an oversupply of apartments on the market."

"I see," I said, thinking I did. I thought for moment and said, "So, rents went down as your property taxes went up?"

"The Squeeze." Walter wrenched his napkin into a twisted knot as if to illustrate his financial setback. He said, "The only way you can make that inverse equation work is to put more money into the property so you can cover that short fall in revenue against an increase in expenses." He hesitated. "Or else you must sell the albatross. That's when you look around, hoping to find the next sucker."

"And did you do that?"

Water nodded. "Like Newfoundland when things weren't working, they punted their whole basket to Canada, as I did my investment to someone else."

I waited and then pressed, "You mentioned Flipper Number Two."

"It was like Labrador tied to Newfoundland. In the merger, it went along for the ride."

CHAPTER 21
UPDATE THE MIND

All of a sudden, still waiting for the evening's speaker, I remembered that a few moments earlier, Walter was about to give me an answer to some question I'd now forgotten about. Maybe he'd forgotten, too, or maybe he'd changed his mind about his answer. Or maybe I knew the answer and didn't want to hear it. But he did give it to me anyway, telling me, "Jerry, you've got to get your mind into the 21st Century—"

"—Thought it was."

"You and a lot of people your age."

"My age? Our age!"

"Some of us are up to speed." Walter laughed and patted my arm in a friendly gesture, so that I knew he wasn't trying to be confrontational or judgmental like some minister in his or her robes carrying out some divine mission of judging people charged to him as members of his congregation, or some judge pounding a gavel from high atop some bench in some court issuing verdicts of justice based on the embrace of the canons of local, state, or federal law. "It's your turn to move forward," he said and smiled.

"Okay, in order for me to get up to speed, you're going to supply the rocket fuel?"

Walter prophesized, "To get you tuned into to today's popular program."

I waited, speculating, but only for an instant, as Walter went on, "Jerry, first, you must get a feeling in your bones and in your mind about the concept of impermanence." He waited for me to give him some sign of staying with him. Unsatisfied with my lack of reply, he added, "You can't hide in the parameters of the past like a lot of folks around here do. They had life figured out forty or fifty years ago, and want to continue to live their lives as if they were back in those days... with those guidelines... but...." Seeing no response, he blurted, "Remember the Neanderthals!"

I looked at him in dismay, but managed to query, "What the hell are you talking about?"

"Exactly my point."

"No, I never knew one of those guys, and I never hope to meet one, let alone remember them."

Walter repeated, "Exactly my point."

"Elucidate," I commanded, as a friend can occasionally take the liberty of commanding a friend. "I suppose you're going to tell me these Neanderthals of yours printed stamps, and you have a set in your obsolete country collection?" From Walter's grimace, I knew I had overstepped myself, and I hastened, "I'm sorry."

"You're getting there," he told me and smiled.

"I'm lost," I said in a bit of a begging tone.

"So is our generation. Like the Lost Generation that huddled in Paris after World War I. Orbiting in their own coffee houses and, well, revolving around their own dimming sun, lost in their own unique and peculiar thoughts. While enjoying the unique fleeting episodes of their own peculiar fun life. Enjoying, their lives, so they thought, in their cocoon, feeling safe from the world outside, the world they were avoiding, dodging, running from. They found themselves in a small and safe field of likeminded escapists...."

I thought I had begun to get the gist. "Meanwhile...."

"Exactly." Walter waited. "Meanwhile back in time, our friends the Neanderthals, were being out-thought and out-maneuvered by the new guys and gals on the block—that's us Homo Sapiens. And so, my friend Jerry, you now have the definition and example for our term and our accompanying reality of impermanence. Once in time the Neanderthals were on top, but all of a sudden—well, it wasn't overnight, of course—they were all going through the exit doors in large groups, wondering why their lives were changing so drastically, indeed being relegated to the specie's dust bin."

Picking up on the gist of his message, I tried, "So, are you saying that you and I, and maybe most of the people here in this community of Macrobia, are the equivalent of yesterday's Lost Generation."

"No, Jerry, those of us who are here today are in the present moments of life. We are today's older generation, the senior citizens of life, even if many of us are still living in the past. We are the present, and to us and to the present, we must yield our mental outlooks, our emotions, our attention. Impermanence is the onslaught coming down the freeway towards us, and passing us with gusto. At or above the speed limit. Impermanence has arrived and will continue to arrive, with its continual changes."

I shuddered at the thought. "Wait a minute," I said so loudly the ladies' conversations at our table came to an abrupt halt as the six women looked at me, perhaps in dismay, perhaps in a gender alert, a warning of sorts, and I promptly apologized out loud to our women table companions, who then promptly took up again whatever their topics of conversation had been before my interruption.

"I'm waiting," I said to Walter. "You want to tell me something?" I hesitated. As the light bulb went on, I added in a low voice, "Oh, you are remembering my beef with the guy who bad mouthed me to the ladies in the political club, effectively banning me from participation in their club?"

Walter nodded, held up his hand and, in no uncertain terms, instructed me, "I told you to forget that guy. Put him on some rear shelf in your mind's closet." He paused and waited for his words to sink in, which they did. I sensed Walter was growing impatient with me. But then he began again, "Now we are going to talk about something more constructive."

In the brief silence, I studied him for a moment. "Wait, Walter. I need to tell you what sort of therapy I had, all those years ago before the grieving therapy I had after my wife Matilda passed away."

Walter waited.

I ventured, "It was therapy supposedly to treat depression, which had overcome me. You see, I couldn't get a job, couldn't earn any money to care for my three kids and my wife. I was damned to failure and descending into the depths of despair. I lived in that dark rabbit hole, burrowing deeper. I was barely hanging on to life."

"What was this special type of therapy, Jerry?"

"Electro shock."

"Jesus." A pause. "You?"

"Yes, for two months, in the…."

"Don't say it."

I didn't.

"And did… I mean, were you… I mean…."

"It was supposed to—given the state of psychiatry in those dim days of yesteryear—clear me of worrisome memories, so that I wouldn't dwell on past failures, re-live past emotions, and that I would then clear my mind of all those bad things. And that would make me whole. It wouldn't necessarily get me a job, but it would prepare me for the proper attitude in which to seek employment." It was my turn to chuckle. "Maybe I would become a perfect person."

"Sounds to me like Buddhist meditation concepts without the electric jolt," Walter said with a voice of familiarity with the general subject.

"Your experience?"

He said, "Indeed, when I was a psychologist. Remember, I told you?" Then he asked, "Did it? I mean, the electro-shock treatments clear your mind of the undesirable burdens of your past self?"

I thought for a moment. "I have no memory of memories that it zapped, if it did do any of that. But today, even at my age, my memory is sharp as a tack. I can remember a lot more—when I open even the remotest file drawer of my mind's file cabinet. They're all there if I choose to take out each file and look through it."

We sat in silence, except that the chatter from the ladies was trumping our quiet mood.

Then Walter went on talking about his oldtime friends, the ancients, "As I was trying to explain, we're the Neanderthals, and your kids and my kids are the homo sapiens. They're soon going to take over, ousting us, or should I say ostracizing us here in this retirement community from our roles as, say, a family head, as patrons or as matrons trying to pursue our perceived duties to our legacy, to our kids, to our community, to society. All that is there only for the genealogists to chronicle, and their re-touching of old photographs to bring them back to life, given their advanced technology. I mean, I suggest you try to forget trying to cohabit the conference room in your restaurant with them, for they are into the new pizza parlor out on the freeway exchange."

I puzzled over Walter's words. I resisted them, resisted Walter. I wanted to give him a knuckle sandwich. I wanted to yell loudly in protest. I wanted to get off this impermanence train, dodge the approaching juggernaut. In despair, I asked, "Communicate with them?" And then, again out loud, I answered my own query, "Try, I suppose, but don't count on being on the same wavelength."

Walter said, "Now we've shared our kid-experiences. There's more, but this is enough for one time."

CHAPTER 22
THE EVENING'S SPEAKER

"You will, Mr. President, have to decide what is good advice."
—Herbert Hoover to J. F. Kennedy at his inauguration

From the podium in the Event Center, Jewell Jones, the club president, waved toward the arriving speaker, whom she saw entering the hall. Jovially, the speaker waved back. Jewell promptly turned on her microphone and announced with glee, "Our speaker has arrived!" She went on to tell her hungry guests, "Dr. Brady will have a bite and then begin her talk on aging."

"We've aged a bit while were sitting here waiting," Lilly said to chirps of agreement from several of the women at our table. Neither Walter nor I said anything, although maybe he agreed with Lilly, and probably I did, too. I said as much to her, to her surprise that I would say anything to her, especially in what I thought was my cordial male voice.

$$* \qquad * \qquad *$$

Jewell was soon introducing the speaker, "We are privileged this evening to have Dr. Yvonne Brady. She is chair of the gerontology laboratory in the think tank that is affiliated with our prestigious state university. With her PhD in psychology from Harvard and her MD from Stanford, Dr. Brady is uniquely qualified to talk to us about the 'Challenges and Opportunities of Aging.' Please join me in welcoming Dr. Brady." Enthusiastic applause ensued.

Dr. Brady began, "I plan to discuss with you four axioms that I hope will help us all understand and be better equipped to cope with aging, a mental and physical process that each of us undergoes on a daily basis.

"First, the physical: Our bodies change, and that's no surprise to you here in Macrobia. The changes are mostly negative—we may begin to experience balance problems that may lead to one or more falls. Secondly, our increased fatigue level impairs our actions. That comes sooner in life than we'd like.

"Then there are the mental issues, and so I say to you that, thirdly, Our mental acumen may wane and we may find ourselves more readily confused, especially when it comes to what we may regard as baffling new rules and fresh ideas in communications, as set upon us by advances in technology. "And fourthly, our memories may begin to play tricks on us, indeed may cause us to forget names and places and concepts that a few months or years ago we had no trouble recalling. To combat what may appear to be such daunting issues, this evening I want to suggest to you the following guidelines: First, be as active socially as you can, with friends, neighbors, and even reach out to meet new people. Participate in one or more of the many clubs I understand you have access to in your community. Secondly, challenge yourself with reading books, as well as tuning into media, reading print publications, or following the Internet. From those sources, explore and allow your curiosity to roam as freely as if you were a cowgirl or cowboy riding your horse across virgin territory."

"Conceptually, I am in agreement with Yvonne." Walter gestured toward the podium. I supported his viewpoint.

Dr. Brady delved into her next topic. "Each of you need to have a doctor of gerontology who monitors your other doctors. Let's face it, friends, getting old is a relatively new field of medical science and medical practice. In the not too distant past, few of us ever got much past 60 or 65. In fact, if you look at the history of medical science and the actuarial tables, most of our ancestors had trouble even getting past age 50. But that was then, and this is now."

She added another new concept, as she advised, "Thirdly, look at your prescriptions. What I mean is, if your grandkids are given new prescriptions with changing levels from the time they are born to, say age 6, their prescriptions will have followed their ages in tandem as their unique medical circumstances change with age."

Nods from listeners. Nods of their experience with children, albeit years ago, except for grandchildren or even great grandchildren occupying current lives.

"But," Dr. Brady said, "I dare say the prescriptions you may have, in dosing and intent, are cast in stone for everyone today who is past age 60. That's not realistic, given the advances in medical research and clinical techniques that are taking place that have advanced medicine in the past decade, changing the parameters of prescription requirements for you seniors. That's why you need to add a gerontologist MD to your medical life."

With that Dr. Brady opened up her discussion, asking for questions from her audience.

$*$ $*$ $*$

The Critique

I do not resent criticism, even when, for the sake of emphasis,
it parts for the time with reality
—Winston Churchill, 1941

The ensuing questions went on for some time, as everyone was vitally interested in the topic of aging. During her talk, I nodded off only once. Walter seemed alert, that is, when I diverted my attention from Yvonne to him. Finally, after the last question, Jewell Jones declared the meeting adjourned, Walter said we should go to my place for a non-alcoholic beer. "Got to keep the alcohol consumption under control," he said, asking, "Didn't she say something about that?" I allowed as how she must have because I recall my doctor voicing a similar admonition.

But instead of leaving the Events Center, we, as did most of the other people, continued to sit there and, among ourselves, review the speaker's talk. Aging was on everyone's minds. I found two O'Douls at the still open bar, and Walter and I sat "for a spell," as my uncle would often invite.

Walter sipped and voiced his inquiry, "Tell me, Jerry, after listening to the talk, what do you make of this retirement life style, or retirement itself and, well… your earlier and younger life that has enabled you to pursue what everyone is calling this new way of life here in Macrobia, that being, simply, 'retirement'?"

"It is what it is." I replied.

"And what is it that it is?" he wanted to know, as if there was a something else, some more things to know, which I didn't really know if there were, really. In this place, did you just take what came, or was there a strategy for living here? Or maybe, I wondered, did we each need to address a whole new list of strategies?

Walter pointed his right index finger at me, almost threatening; no, it was in a get ready to receive a pontification. I mean, as if he were saying, get ready, for it may be long.

"You go, then," I suggested, "you answer your question." I suspected that's what he wanted to do anyway.

Walter nodded. Once more he said, "Here's my take…."

"On this place?"

He nodded. "As well as my take on retirement." He waited for my attention and then continued, "Our Macrobia is a by-product of the burgeoning forces of those of us actually in retirement. The concept is what the media continually writes and talks about. And the reason for their attention is that younger and middle-aged reporters are— each of them—worried about what they should do with their own aging parents. These reporters and commentators are also fixated on how their own future retirement care is going to be saved up for and then paid for by them. They are continually asking themselves and financial experts if they will have enough money set aside? On top of these journalistic concerns, come their own family worries of how they are going to face the costs of college education for their kids, and on top of that come worries about how they are going to deal with the rise in their own medical insurance premiums." Walter took a breath and added, "In my opinion, the media people are compelled to report on the entire topic of aging by citing as many popular stereotypes that they hear, recall, and recite."

"And?"

"So, Jerry, we get a basket of partial truths combined with misinformation from the biases of younger-in-age writers and commentators. It is their pattern to repeat what 'everyone knows' as far as age and aging is concerned. And, believe me, every one of them does not know jack, unless they are here in person with us and walking in our moccasins."

Prodding my friend, I asked, "So, what is your game plan? I man, our game plan? You and me?

He showed a hint of annoyance, as Walter can do and does from time to time, and as I've seen him do with others. His is a short fuse, as they say in the electric business. Well, I don't really know what they say in the electric business, for I've never been charged with looking into it, so I elected to simply wait and listen for my friend's words, which I dutifully did.

"Jerry, you and I, plus most of the males here I've talked to have been lured—maybe I should say trapped—into a lifestyle that benefits most of the few people running our society."

"Walter, what are you saying."

"Hear me out."

"I will, go on."

Walter did. "We males—"

"—That's us."

"Are trained, conditioned from an early age to seek out a career, a job, so that we can get married, so that when we impregnate a woman, the resultant child is what they call "legitimate" and entitled to society's benefits of legality when it comes to inheritance of property rights."

"Right on," I underlined, recalling with pain my own pre-marital lark.

Walter continued, "That male scenario entails getting an education, either in college or in training programs, and it brings with it a routine of working day after day in a job that will, or promises, to pay out an eventual retirement benefit in the form of a pension. That benefit then becomes suitable for us to qualify to get into a place like Macrobia." With both hands, he gestured around.

I asked, "But do we males, regardless of our origin, that is, our birthplace, or our birth family, ever have a choice in designing our lives? Or are we branded from birth with a scarlet 'D' for duty to our future family, or our existing family, or the lineage of our existing family tree, back to past generations?"

Walter smiled at me. For effect, he waited and then replied, "Damn right we have choices! But due to societal pressure—and then there's the pressure from our woman to get a job, become gainfully employed, as that source of income as administered by us promises her financial support when she has her baby or babies. On the other hand, if we never take this authorized official male course, with its authorized and approved male characteristics, then we won't, or can't, or don't end up—years later—in a retirement place such as Macrobia."

I protested, "I don't consider myself 'ending up' here."

"You goin' someplace else in your old age?"

I laughed and said I had no nascent plans.

"Well, then heed what I'm explaining about you, me, and all the other males living here, or who want to live here, or who someday will want to live here."

I laughed at Walter. "Okay, my friend, you're saying that from the day we're born, we're predestined to eventually inhabit a place like Macrobia?"

He asked, "Is it likely? Not without a pension or a big nest egg. You're not going to pass the money test to make it in here, and if you don't have that big pension, you're goin' someplace else less attractive, that is, if you're goin' anywhere at all other than on your couch as a potato, if you've even got a couch to potato on."

"So, if I choose an alternative lifestyle, I'm sunk?"

Walter said, "Yes, unless you, like me, hit some sort of a jackpot or lottery or happen to build your house on a mother lode of gold or atop a field rich in lithium or some other valuable rare earth that is in short supply."

I said, "Wait a minute. Suppose I decide that I value quality of life above a job with a large organization that may or may not stifle me in expression of my ideas and my drive and my whatever else I think I have that is of benefit to me and fun for me in my life?"

"Apart from putting yourself in the category of one of my derelict countries in my stamp collection in which I value the ones who don't make it, you'll be like my friends in Epirus—back to being a person in a position without benefits. Maybe, and I don't say that because I know, only because the real pension-type benefits usually come from big organizations, whether corporate, non-profit, or government."

I asked, "Can you and I name some of the male alternatives?"

"Why?" Walter exclaimed, telling me, "That would be an exercise in futility."

I didn't heed my friend and went on, speculating, "I could have become a monk, lived in a remote monastery all my life, benefited from being part of such an organization, all the while being provided for. I would have led a spiritual life, cloistered in the sanctuary of common beliefs of my peers, reading and studying and reciting and chanting with them, researching all the topics of importance in the world, studying and enjoying camaraderie with other males who were following a similar lifetime bent."

Walter laughed. "Living there, Jerry, you would have no women to contend with."

"Probably why I didn't choose that course in life."

Walter and I remained silent for a while, perhaps in thought, perhaps adrift in recalling the paths our lives have taken us, or we have taken them.

Soon Walter suggested he and I might talk about gender differences. He added, "There are value differences, as well."

I urged, "You're on."

Hesitatingly, he began, "It's quite basic, so it seems to me; I mean, the biological differences—I mean, these are basics for beginners wishing to explore the gender topic."

I concurred that most of us were on board up to this point. "So, go deeper, my friend, if you will, or can, or want to."

He said he would, and continued with, "That leads us into the hormones."

"Uh huh."

"They're different."

"I believe that is a truism."

"As such, they wiggle their way into our minds."

I went along by recalling Walter's conversation with the six ladies at our table about the urge and desire and even drive to make money when we were younger, and even older. I said as much to my friend, to which he nodded, "That experience with them tells us quite a bit more."

"How so?"

Walter thought a bit. As I have found out, he was not accustomed to making snap judgments, at least out loud, though he may have made them in his mind but was reluctant to blurt them out. Soon, he said, no rather suggested, for his tone was more inquisitive than dogmatic, "Women," he began in his attempt to broad brush the gender, with which I immediately, to myself, quarreled, "are not comfortable with change. They would like things to stay pretty much the same in their lives—take their regard for family and the place where they live—their nest. Oh, they may change the kitchen curtains from time to time, but that's not real change, that's simply enhancement."

"And men?"

"We, you and I, and most men, live with change, are accustomed to dealing with it, thrive in the new solutions that must be devised in order to try to cope with change in society and in business. Making money and the desire to do so entails change, for the economy is changing, and men must keep up with those changes if they are to make the right investment decisions, whether it's investment of money or investment of their effort and their time."

Agreeing, I suggested, "Many of us senior men have to unlearn a lot of things in this third half of our lives—that is, if we are going to learn new things." Then I asked, "But what about women?"

Walter thought for a moment before he said, "They eschew change, seek a scenario that's more or less fixed. I mean, I think it stems from the characteristics of the gestation period and the intimate time they cherish and spend with a new born, and bless them for these traits, for without them, few of us would be here today."

I asked Walter, "Have you ever shared these thoughts with a woman?"

"Well, yes, and my late wife told me that in the ultimate moments of childbirth, the endorphins were racing in her mind with the fantastic stimulation she was deriving from the endurance event. She said during those moments she saw the universe in its beauty and the world we're on in its magnificence. She told me that she wanted to remain in that state of euphoria indefinitely. After her six nirvana experiences, at least for a while, she confessed to me that she abhorred change."

"Yes, you told me you had six... well... I mean your four plus two."

Walter nodded. "Each time, the same. Maybe that's why she had six. Six natural endorphin stimulated highs."

"Meanwhile? You?"

"I was changing jobs, changing careers, adding to my stamp collection, changing my focus in life, and I'm still changing my orientation to life. I'm change personified, while she was content in the comfort of her environment. She told me so once."

"Maybe it goes back to the hunter-gatherers," I opined. "Men hunted and had to change their positions and their attack plans on the mammoths and those other big targets; it was a necessity of survival..."

"...Meanwhile, the women were back in the village with their children grinding corn and acorns in a changeless society."

We laughed together. I said, "Maybe we should try out your gender theory the next time we're at a dinner table with six women."

Chapter 23
The Daughter?

Suffer the little children to come unto me, and forbid them not…
—St. Mark, 10:14

From outside the Event Center came the shrill sound of a paramedics' fire engine, followed by the chorus of an ambulance's two-tier sirens. While these were not unfamiliar Marcrobian sounds, this intrusion on the folks in the hall was unwelcome. I looked up to see the emergency vehicles' lights and warning sounds coming through the building's glass entry doors.

At that moment, a guy I had once sat next to at some sporting event came up to me, putting his hand firmly on my shoulder, and said, "Hey, Gerald—"

"—Jerry—"

"—Yeah… didn't you tell me you were from Indiana?"

I nodded.

He kneeled by my side and whispered, "I'm Roger."

"Yes." I smiled. "I remember."

"Well, the ambulance has come to collect a woman I know slightly…."

"The ambulance?"

He nodded. "She and I talked once. She told me her father was from Indiana. No one else around here is from that place, so that's why I remember her telling me. It was so unusual. I thought maybe you might know her or, more likely, her father. But now, she's in the ambulance, and going off to the ER."

I was stunned. I suggested, "There's no one else here from Indiana. Except me."

135

"She's from New York."

Listening, Walter looked at me. Sternly, he instructed, "Go."

I did.

"What's her name?" I asked the paramedic, who was impatient to close the rear door of the ambulance.

She told me.

"My God!" I looked into the ambulance and, stunned, said profoundly to the paramedic, "I'm her father."

"You?" she replied incredulously.

"I'm sure."

"Climb in and ride with us to the ER." She whispered, "She may not have long."

I managed the maneuver.

From off the gurney, she looked at me. Was there recognition? I was still in sort of a state of shock. "You moved here? To Macrobia?" I asked her.

Slowly she nodded.

The paramedic whispered to me, "Her husband passed away recently. I remember the emergency call for him."

"Anna," I said, speaking her name for the first time in how many years? Was it, and I tried to calculate, 60... 63... 67...?

A slight smile from her as the ambulance started up, its blue and red lights flashing. As we drove away from the Event Center entrance, I saw Walter, a look of concern dominating his countenance.

He and I would have a lot more to talk about on the morrow.

CHAPTER 24
WRITING ABOUT A ROOM OF ONE'S OWN

I will make you brooches and toys for your delight
Of bird-song at morning and star-shine at night
I will make a palace fit for you and me
Of green days in forests and blue days at sea
I will make my kitchen, and you shall keep your room
Where white flows the river and bright blows the broom
And you shall wash your linen and keep your body well
In rainfall at morning and dewfall at night
—Robert Louis Stevenson

In Macrobia, I had discovered a secret place offering sanctuary. It was just right for me. Goodness knows, I need such a refuge to go to, virtually every day, at least for a few minutes, maybe only 30 or so, if only to re-orient myself back to the basics of age, that is, being here in Macrobia. Every time I retreated there to meditate, I would remind myself that I must get along with the constant buzz of club activities, converse with the people I happen to meet, and try to participate in events beyond the stamp club where I would no longer be talking only to my friend Walter.

Not helping me to assimilate in this community is my lack of skill in befriending male friends among the small number that actually live here. Unless I'm at a sporting event, sitting in the stands amidst a bunch of guys, simply discovering where the men are, or even one man, in a place like this—yes, just finding them—is a task in itself. Once found, then how do you start a significant conversation other than to talk about a football or basketball score, or the latest in automobile design or engine power, or heaven forbid, telling an off-color joke, although I don't know many, and that is a handicap here for sure. Maybe after I'm here a decade I will have accumulated enough experience in sports and car motors and design, and oh yes, off-color jokes, to be able to initiate and cultivate a normal, typical, run-of-the-mill male conversation. Not bonding. Not deep. Surface, I call it.

As to my retreat, thinking about it over time, I composed this summary of my feelings in my new writing journal. I want to add that I am finding a new horizon to life as I compose entries for my writing journal. So, here goes my entry:

My special retreat is a place where I go, sometimes daily, sometimes not at all. I know it is always there, and I know, if I need to, I can seek refuge in its sense of remote safety, a sense apart from all else, a sense of me, perhaps, a reassurance that I am me and not simply a bit player on the stage of life, here on this playground of retirement, but a precious human being that every morning welcomes the day, or tries to, and rejoices that I am still alive and reasonably well in health, given my advanced years of aging. After parting from Walter and returning from the ER later that evening following the passing of my daughter, that's where I went, not to my little home, but there, thinking out loud, "Now for sure, there is no more immediate family in my life… just me."

I had discovered the loft—my retreat—while exploring the old stagecoach stop. It was up a short flight of narrow stairs. The décor was, well, old, and antique California. There's not much really old in California other than a small number of Native American sites, some still in the charge of the extant tribal governance.

Mounted on one wall of my retreat, someone had hung a rendering of the Buddha; next to him was a framed portrait of the Dalai Lama. There was a small chair in front of the two, and that is where I usually sat. In silence. You could say in meditation, trying to clear my mind of myself, while struggling and yearning to find my true self.

I reasoned that if I could clear my mind, rid it of useless clutter, of anxiety about myself and my children and grandchildren, even though the members were far apart, then I would not worry about my medical future, or feel fright about my finances, and hopefully I would begin to see, underneath and beyond all the removed debris, in a welcome fresh look, there would be revealed my true self.

Of course, the older one becomes, the more there seems to be a cluttering of the mind. Memories of people. Memoires of past events. Memories of mistakes. Memories of places lived. Memories of happy times. Wonderful memories. Painful memories.

Sitting for a period of time there in my special place I found I was able to launch a mental beginning. The sufferings of the past, and sometimes the present that I was experiencing, might soon leave, and a warm feeling would replace it as I took on a fresh look about myself, and my surroundings. I began to feel I could respect the people I might meet in this community. I have never told Walter about this special room.

Two candleholders with thick white candles shown soft light, while a single dangling light bulb with an old switch above the bulb added the reality of a later but now old old technology. I'd usually light the candles and savor the glow and the shadows. If it were night, I'd also switch on the electric bulb.

Sometimes I would bring my album of postage stamps displaying countries that exist today, and remind myself that I, too, exist today. I was not a failed nation, like the stamps Walter collected. Nor am I a failed person. I have not been cancelled by a postmark, but instead I am a warm, live human being, ready to communicate with the world today, not stuck in the past of yesteryear.

Later on, I did confide to Walter about my special retreat and how I felt about it. I made an attempt to describe the relief being there often brought to me. There it was, as I tried to reveal my feelings of being there, a certain relief in solitude, a relief of being alone, a relief of not hearing others chattering, that is, until I heard people down below talking—sometimes women in their higher tones, but usually men in their deeper voices. Being alone there meant I was on my own, no schedule, no deadline, no pressure.

Walter listened politely, no intently, I was sure. He was my friend and he was interested in what I was doing. Then he began to describe to me his own retreat. It was at some distance, toward the ocean. It was a Zen Buddhist place, a garden where they grew their own vegetables and fruits and prepared their own meals. But it was also a place of meditation, given the environmental benefits of peace, tranquility, and dedication to a common philosophy on the part of those there. He said he went there a couple times a year for a week or so just to be in tune with himself and with the world, to feel the compassion of the others who worked there or went there from time to time with the same mission in mind as his.

"How do you feel when you return?" I asked.

"Like I'm still there in my mind—the residual feeling lasts and lasts." He went on to tell me, "Often I wish Macrobia was like that place of mine."

THE EPILOGUE JERRY HAS WRITTEN

So, it is for you, Dear Reader, to ask me, "Who are you, the person who sets these words to paper, reports on the world of aging, and who thinks these and other thoughts?" Fair enough. Here is my Epilogue:

*   *   *

There is an old hall, a quiet secluded place, where persons retreat to meditate. It is within sight of the Pacific Ocean but, of course, once inside one no longer sees the ocean. Nor the sunset, whose rays march up the green valley in a message of wholeness, for the garden itself and for the persons who walk within it, or for the persons who prepare the organic food, or for the persons who bow before and after and remain silent while consuming the nourishment. Silent, that is, until after the spell of some 15 minute of silence.

Prior, and following the hour or so of meditation the chants to the Buddha are in English, followed by Japanese, for this Zen center traces its intellectual lineage to the Buddhism of Japan, following its genesis in Tibet, or was it in India? Maybe original, or like most spiritual beliefs, emanating from out of the mist of past events, from older people, old even then, the telling down through multiple generations with earlier thoughts, ideas, tales, legends, writings, hopes, and fears.

*   *   *

It was here that Walter insisted we go, and remain for a week of being with the garden, the sunsets, the camaraderie of those who meditate. And it is here we went, toward the Pacific Ocean.

There is a certain peace of the Pacific, in peacetime, and after all, we were

141

living in the peacetime that followed those many years ago of that awful wartime, of which Walter and I and so many others of our age can still remember, whether we were in it, or watching from its fringes. But now was peacetime, here in the green valley.

And silence in the large meditation chamber—silence for the hour or so. Silence in which one's life can pass, or more biting to experience, oneself can be felt. Who am I, this person? Where have I come from? Where am I now? And where am I going? Or does it matter in the scheme of self? And what is the self?

Is the soul the self? Is the person the self? Is the ego the self? Or is the self an opportunity to explore the self? Walter said that if we meditated enough, we would stumble upon the answers. And what is enough time, how many sessions? How many walks in the garden, how many evenings in the sunset's waning rays, its orangeness dropping down beyond the rim of the ocean, we watching, silently, my mind turning inward? Or outward? Or not at all?

And so I thought about myself. And I thought about the others I had known, the others I knew, Matilda and those in my family. My newly-deceased daughter and seeing her after all those years. And again, about myself. Those for whom I had compassion, and I realized I should have compassion for all sentient begins, and I also realized the immensity of such a broad and all-consuming philosophy. I doubted I was capable of such a mission with my life. But I told myself I should try and try hard, for Walter had said that there was hope of enlightenment at the end of such a road. So, I vowed to try, to make the attempt, especially when I returned to Macrobia. There, there were so many people, so many lives, so many careers, so many bases, so many beliefs, such a volume of lives lived, and now still being lived, and still to be experienced. So much mental stuff to inhale. So exciting.

Yes, I assured my friend Walter, I would try to understand.

THE END

ABOUT THE AUTHOR

A native of Indiana, Jon Foyt began writing novels and screenplays with his late wife, Lois Foyt, in 1992. A distance runner, he has finished 60 marathons. He holds degrees from Stanford in Journalism and Geography plus an MBA. He has completed class work for an Historic Preservation masters at the University of Georgia.

Foyt's other careers have included radio broadcasting, banking, and real estate development in Oregon and California. At 87, Jon is an active participant in the retirement community of Rossmoor in Walnut Creek, California. He has three children, eight grandchildren, and two great-grandsons.

OTHER WORKS BY THE AUTHOR

204881R00085

Made in the USA
Columbia, SC
07 May 2019